True Love At Last?

"Ooh, Louie! That tickles!" I heard Ellen giggle. "Hold my hand, don't play with it!" My heart dropped.

So this was it. I had wanted proof of how Louie felt, and now I had it. He was obviously choosing Ellen over me. Tears burned my eyes. I tried sniffling them back, but they kept on coming.

I don't know if Louie heard me crying or just sensed that I was upset. But at that moment his hand touched my shoulder. Then his arm went around me.

I couldn't believe it! I quickly wiped my eyes and snuggled up to him. It was the most wonderful feeling to be so close to Louie. He must like me. He must!

Louie's face was right up against mine. I was afraid to breathe. Was he finally going to kiss me?

Books by Linda Lewis

IS THERE LIFE AFTER BOYS?
WE HATE EVERYTHING BUT BOYS
WE LOVE ONLY OLDER BOYS

Available from ARCHWAY paperbacks

WE LOVE ONLY OLDER BOYS

LINDA LEWIS

AN ARCHWAY PAPERBACK
Published by POCKET BOOKS • NEW YORK

AN ARCHWAY PAPERBACK *Original*

An Archway Paperback published by
POCKET BOOKS, a division of Simon & Schuster Inc.
1230 Avenue of the Americas, New York, NY 10020

ISBN: 0-671-64916-7

First Archway Paperback printing February 1988

10 9 8 7 6 5 4 3 2

AN ARCHWAY PAPERBACK and colophon are registered trademarks of Simon & Schuster Inc.

Printed in the U.S.A.

IL 5+

To Joyce and Kenny—
the best to come
from me and Lenny

WE LOVE ONLY OLDER BOYS

Chapter One

ONE THING I'VE noticed about life; it's filled with all sorts of surprises. The littlest incident—a change of plans, a chance meeting—can start a whole chain reaction of things happening. Before you know it, your life has changed and will never be the same again.

That was just what happened the day Jan Zieglebaum and I decided to take the subway home from Huntington, the school we go to, instead of our customary bus. There, in the very car we wound up in, was sitting none other than the great Sheldon Emory. And it was that chance meeting that really started everything.

To understand the importance of all this, you have to know what is so great about Sheldon. He's sixteen years old and absolutely gorgeous! Not only that, but I get the credit for having discovered him in the first place. It was way back when I was in sixth grade, and still having silly crushes on immature boys my own age, that I spotted Sheldon playing baseball in the park.

He was so good looking he absolutely took my breath away. I watched him running, tossing his head to flip away the thick black hair that flopped forward into his eyes. I saw him scoop up the ball and skillfully fire it to home plate in time to get the batter out, his strong muscles rippling under his T-shirt. Then I heard him yell in victory, with an adorable crackling in his voice that had already started to change.

His voice made me realize that, even though he was short, he had to be older than I was. It turned out he was three years older—too old to be interested in a girl just turning twelve. But now that my friends and I were past thirteen and official teenagers, three years didn't seem like so much. We found the boys our own age, whom we used to like, to be too immature and babyish for us now. We were interested in older boys—boys fifteen and sixteen years old to be exact—boys like Sheldon. We figured they should be interested in us, too.

Unfortunately, Sheldon did not yet seem to be aware of this fact. Oh, he graced us with a few words now and then, or threw us a quick smile. But that was about it. Obviously, we were still just cute little girls to him instead of girlfriend material. Something had to happen sometime to change all that. And maybe that sometime was now.

"Look, Jan, there's Sheldon!" I whispered excitedly. "And there are two empty seats next to him. Let's go sit in them!"

"Sit? Next to Sheldon?" Jan's brown eyes widened and seemed to fill her tiny face. "B-but then we'll have to TALK to him. And w-what are we going to say?"

"We'll find something," I said with more confidence than I felt. After all, I don't think I'd ever said more than two or three sentences at a time to Sheldon. And it had always been at times when there were other kids around. To carry on a conversation with him on the whole ride home meant thinking up twenty-two minutes' worth of things to say. It would be pretty embarrassing to run out in the middle of the trip!

"Okay, Linda, it's up to you," said Jan. So she followed me through the car as I made my way toward where Sheldon was sitting.

That's the way it always was with Jan and me. She was always looking up to me to take the lead and give her courage.

Jan was only a few months younger than I was, but she looked more like eight or nine than almost thirteen. With her big brown eyes and her brown hair cut like a pixie's, Jan was actually cute, in a mouselike kind of way. But she was also skinny, completely flatchested, and shy, and boys never seemed to be aware that she was around.

For me, fortunately, it was different. Although I'm not much taller than Jan, my body at least has started to develop. My figure is in proportion, and my shoulder-length light brown hair is nice and thick. And while my nose that's one size too big for my face absolutely ruins my looks, as far as I'm concerned, people tell me that my big blue eyes more than make up for it.

3

At any rate, I've at least had some limited success with boys. In sixth grade there was Jeff, but that relationship died a slow, torturous death when we wound up going to different junior high schools. Then, last year, I fell for Mark, the first older boy to pay enough attention to me to make me feel important. Not important enough, however. Over the summer, Mark met another girl when he was away in the country. He wound up going steady with her, and that was the end of our relationship.

So here it was, a new school year. Jan and I were in eighth grade, and Sheldon, who was sixteen, adorable, and had lots of cute friends as well, was prime boyfriend material. And here we were, with a perfect opportunity to get something going by talking to him on the train.

I took a deep breath and started making my way toward where Sheldon was sitting. Jan followed slowly behind me. Sheldon was engrossed in some math textbook and didn't even notice we were there.

I stood in front of him for a second, trying to come up with some cool and clever introductory remark. Then, without warning, the A train stopped short in the station. This caused me to lurch forward and lose my balance. My books dropped to the floor, and I wound up sitting in a startled Sheldon's lap. Jan wound up down on her knees, leaning on top of me for support.

"Hey! What's going on here?" was Sheldon's angry reaction.

"Sorry, Sheldon. It was the darn train," I apologized. I pushed Jan off me and struggled to my feet. I busied myself with picking up my books and papers as fast as I could. I didn't want him to see that my face was burning with embarrassment. And to think I had been trying to look cool!

"Well, if it isn't Linda Berman," Sheldon said, letting out a big laugh at my predicament. "And little Jan. What are you girls doing on this train anyhow?"

"Coming home from school—just like you!" I explained as I stuffed my papers back into my looseleaf. I brushed myself off and sat down in the seat next to him. Jan plopped down beside me, gazing at Sheldon through love-glazed eyes.

"Oh. How come I never ran into you on the train before?" Sheldon asked logically as the train started up again.

"We usually take the bus," I explained, placing my books on my knees where I hoped they would stay put. "But we went to our club after school today. It's at the Manhattan School for the Blind, and from there it's easier to take the train."

"School for the Blind? Why do you have a club there?"

I was surprised that Sheldon was interested enough in our activities to bother asking. But since he had, I took full advantage of the opportunity to keep the conversation going. I explained all about the service club at our school, Huntington, that did volunteer work at the Manhattan School helping out with the blind kids. I told him Jan and I worked with the

Manhattan School's art club, since we were both good in art.

"Art—huh?" Sheldon didn't look too excited. "I'm not much good at art, myself."

"Well, we can't be good at everything," I said. "And after all, you're so-o-o good at sports."

"Yeah? You think so?" Sheldon positively beamed. Then he went into this long description of how the team he and his friends played on, the Royals, would soon be taking part in the baseball finals, and how his position, shortstop, was so important.

I listened to Sheldon as if what he was saying was the most fascinating bit of information in the world. When I first started liking older boys, my father had given me a piece of advice I always tried to keep in mind. When talking to someone else, it was important to pay attention to and be interested in what they were saying. If you didn't and just started thinking of yourself and what you were going to say next, the chances were you'd wind up all self-conscious and self-centered, and mess up the conversation anyway. It was better to just relax, listen, and be yourself.

So that's what I tried to do with Sheldon. It must have worked. Because from talking about baseball, we went on to talk about sports that guys and girls could all do together. We decided one of the best was ice skating.

"It's the one sport where size and strength doesn't matter," I told him. "Girls can skate as well as any boy."

"I don't know about that," he grinned impishly,

showing a full mouth of braces that, on him, actually looked cute. "I've only ice skated a few times, myself. But I bet after a little practice, I'd be as good as any of you girls who've been ice skating for years."

"Oh yeah?" I felt my face flash angrily at that. It made me furious when boys acted so darn superior! "I'd love to take you up on that one, Sheldon. My friends and I will meet you and your friends at the skating rink any time you like. Then we'll see who are the better skaters!"

Sheldon laughed, and I noticed his eyes were not brown, but hazel, flecked with specks of green and yellow. "I'll accept your challenge, Linda. In fact, I just heard that the rink in Central Park is opening up soon for the season. Why don't you get a few friends together, and so will I. We'll show you girls that boys are just naturally better at everything!"

"I can't wait to prove you wrong, Sheldon. It's a deal!" I extended my hand out to him. He grabbed it, then sprang up and pulled me to my feet. "Hey, what do you think you're doing?" I demanded.

He laughed again. "I just thought you might want to get up now, Linda. This is our stop you know!"

Jan and I waited until Sheldon took off in the direction of his house. Then we grabbed each other and jumped up and down with joy. We had a date with Sheldon! It was practically too wonderful to be true! Wait until we told our friends, Roz and Fran, about this one!

Chapter Two

ALONG WITH JAN and I, Rosalie Buttons (better known as Roz) and Fran Zaro formed a group we called the Gruesome Four. Why the Gruesome Four? Well, when you're twelve years old, feeling awkward and ugly, and are unable to get anywhere with older boys, it's easy to start feeling gruesome. At any rate, one day last year when everything was going wrong, I came up with the name, and it stuck.

Fortunately, we don't feel gruesome most of the time. As a matter of fact, I really don't think we're gruesome at all.

Roz actually is pretty, with long sand-colored hair and eyes that match. Not only that, she's got an older sister who teaches her stuff like how to put on make-up and dress, and how to act around older boys. So Roz does pretty well for herself.

As for Fran, well, she's kind of weird looking with her frizzy black hair, freckled face, and thick glasses.

But when she takes her glasses off so you can see her violet eyes, you suddenly realize that Fran is pretty, too. Anyhow, whenever the four of us get together, you can be sure that something is bound to happen.

Roz practically flipped out when I told her the news about the date with Sheldon. Although it was I who originally discovered him, it was Roz and Jan who really fell for him in a big way. While Fran and I had been involved with Mark and his friend, Gary, Roz and Jan had invested many hours trying to get Sheldon to notice them. But Sheldon had always given the impression that we were nothing more than cute little girls. Until now that is.

On the day of the big ice-skating date, we waited with nervous anticipation for Sheldon to show up at our appointed meeting place. This was at the park wall that overlooked the baseball field—the very spot where I had discovered Sheldon in the first place.

The park was always a meeting place for kids in our neighborhood. Washington Heights, the part of New York City where we lived, was full of apartment buildings, most five and six stories high. The park was a wonderful area of grass and trees that overlooked the Hudson River, where we could forget we were in the city. But the most wonderful part of it had to be the baseball field. Because in it could always be found an assortment of wonderful boys.

"I wonder who Sheldon's going to bring with him," Fran said excitedly, as she climbed up to sit on the wall. "I hope they're all cute!"

"Me, too," I agreed. "We need some new blood

9

around!'' Ever since things burned out with Fran and me and Mark and Gary, the two of us hadn't been able to find anyone to like, much less to like us back.

''Well, don't look now, Linda. But if you're counting on this date to get you acquainted with some new boys, you're going to be sadly disappointed,'' said Roz, pointing down the block.

I looked where she indicated, and my hopes fell. Because walking next to Sheldon was just one other boy.

''Norman Banner,'' Fran said disappointedly. ''What a waste! He hardly counts as a boy at all!''

''I know,'' I said glumly. For we all knew Norman from hanging around the baseball field. Despite his glasses, he really wasn't bad looking. But Norman had one big fault. All he ever thought about was sports. He was quiet and shy when it came to girls. Going on a date with Sheldon and Norman was like going on a date with Sheldon by himself.

We tried not to let our disappointment show. But Sheldon must have picked up on our feelings because no sooner had we sat down on the A train that was to take us downtown than he announced, ''I told some of the rest of the guys about the skating today. Everyone else was too lazy to get up this early, but a few of them may show up at the rink later on.''

''A few?'' Fran and I looked at each other and our spirits picked up. Maybe this day wasn't going to be a waste after all!

When we finally got out on the ice I found myself having a hard time getting used to skating again. My ankles were wobbly so I had to stay near the railing where I had something to grab on to when I lost my balance.

Sheldon and Norman were having no such problems. In no time at all they were zooming around the rink. They were both better skaters than I had thought they would be. I was sorry to see that when it came to speed they were way ahead of us girls.

But not when it came to finesse. That's where Roz stood out. Her parents had given her professional skating lessons and it showed. She whirled around doing all sorts of fancy spins and maneuvers. Sheldon kept watching her, and he looked very impressed with what he saw. Then he actually put aside his masculine pride and asked her to teach him to skate backwards!

"Sure! Just hang on to me!" Roz's face positively glowed as she took hold of Sheldon's hands and spun him around. She pushed forward while he slid backward awkwardly. Roz was definitely making progress with him.

As for me, I was making no progress at all. I struggled out to the middle of the rink where I finally began to pick up speed. I was determined to show Sheldon and Norman that I was a decent enough skater in my own right. I had just caught up to where Roz and Sheldon were skating when someone came slamming into me from behind. I felt my feet sliding out from under me and struggled wildly to regain my balance. It did no good. Thump! I landed flat on my backside in a hard, wet, and slushy portion of the ice.

"Why don't you watch where you're going, Linda Berman?" a voice called out nastily.

I looked up and saw a boy laughing at me as if my sitting there sprawled out on the ice was the funniest sight he'd ever seen. He was the boy who had rammed into me in the first place, and he was a boy who, unfortunately, I had seen before.

He was Lenny Lipoff, who had to have the biggest, loudest, nastiest mouth in the entire neighborhood. Lenny was the type of kid who loved to make trouble. He was wild and crazy, and you never knew what he was going to do next.

Like ramming into me in the skating rink. I just knew Lenny had done it on purpose! Now, here he was, laughing at me and making me look like a fool in front of all my friends, who had gathered around.

I felt my face flush with anger. "Why you rotten— you did that on purpose, Lenny Lipoff. I know you did!"

"Who me? How could you say that, Linda?" The look on Lenny's face was one of pure innocence. "It was an accident—I merely lost my balance. Here, let me help you to your feet." With exaggerated politeness, he reached out his hand to help me up.

And I was dumb enough to give him the benefit of the doubt and let him! I gave him my hand, and he pulled me up to my feet. Only, no sooner had I started to get my balance than he gave my hand a jerk and then let go. Before I knew what was happening, there I was sprawling on the ice again!

Somehow, everyone found this to be very amusing.

All my friends, plus Sheldon, Norman, and Lenny, were practically rolling with laughter, while I was burning with rage. I scooped up a handful of wet slush and tossed it at Lenny. I missed and he went skating around the rink, still laughing away.

"I'll get even with you later, Lenny the Lip," I shouted. "You better not feel safe here for even one second!"

But now I was so angry I couldn't even get up on my feet. I kept slipping and sliding and falling back down again.

"Here, Linda. I'll help you up," a voice boomed out. Two huge hands grabbed me under my arms, lifted me up into the air as if I weighed nothing, and planted me firmly on my feet. I turned around in amazement and saw it was Nicky James, the only person I knew who was capable of a feat like that.

Nicky was the biggest kid in the neighborhood. He was over six feet tall, with feet that were at least size thirteen and hands to match. Nicky had grown over six inches in one year and still hadn't gotten used to it. He was gawky and all out of proportion, with stick-out ears, a hawk nose, and freckles all over his face. But despite his appearance, Nicky was really nice— that is unless you made the mistake of calling him "Glick." No one knew where that nickname came from, but whenever Nicky heard it he would absolutely flip out. But ordinarily, he was very nice—not like that awful Lenny!

"Thanks, Nicky," I said sheepishly, brushing the slush off the seat of my pants. "At least someone around here has some manners!" I glared at Sheldon and Norman, who were now struggling to control their laughter. "What are you doing here, anyhow?"

"Ice skating!" Nicky answered brightly. "Sheldon told us he was coming here with you girls and invited us to come along."

"Sheldon! You invited Lenny Lipoff?!" I turned on Sheldon with anger. "How could you? Of all the boys in the neighborhood! I thought you were going to ask someone nice!"

"Lenny *is* nice—just a little high-spirited," laughed Sheldon. "You just don't know him like I do!"

"And I hope I never will!" I retorted as I skated away. My mind was busy thinking up a scheme to get even with that horrid Lenny Lipoff!

Actually, as much as I hate to admit it, Lenny Lipoff was cute in a funny sort of way. He had thick curly brown hair that tumbled over his forehead and big brown eyes fringed with long straight lashes. He also had a great nose, a feature I alway noticed on people since I was so unhappy with my own. But what made Lenny really interesting looking was the long scar on the right side of his face.

Lenny claimed he got the scar in a knife fight. I didn't believe him for a minute. Although there probably were plenty of people who felt like stabbing Lenny when he opened his big fresh mouth or pulled one of his nasty practical jokes!

Myself included, I fumed, as I skated through the crowd trying to spot him. But Lenny was nowhere on the rink. Where could he have gone?

Then I happened to glance into the rink's snack bar. There was Lenny, standing at the counter busily stuffing his face. On his plate I could see two hot dogs covered with mustard and mounds of sauerkraut. There was a big pile of french fries smothered with ketchup. He had a big cup of soda in one hand. Lenny was totally engrossed in what he was eating, and he had his back to the rink.

I saw my opportunity. I skated off the ice and made my way to the snack bar as quietly as possible. Balancing on the thin blades of my skates, I crept up behind him. I waited until he was about to take a drink of soda. Then I pretended to lose my balance and went crashing into him.

It was beautiful! Not only did his soda slosh up out of the cup and splash all over his food and the table, but he fell forward with his face landing in his plate. When he stood up, there was mustard, ketchup, and sauerkraut stuck all over his face! I loved it!

I forced myself to contain my laughter. "Oh, Lenny! How clumsy of me to trip over my feet that way! Here, let me help you!" I grabbed a handful of napkins and started mopping up the table and dabbing at his face. Of course I only succeeded in smearing the mess even more.

Lenny was truly a sight to behold. Then, just at that moment, the rest of our group showed up at the snack bar. What a triumph it was for me to have them see Lenny standing there with food dripping off his face!

I think if Lenny could have grabbed hold of me, he would have killed me right there and then. But fortunately, he was too busy cleaning himself off. Or maybe he was too embarrassed to show how upset I'd gotten him in front of his friends, who were trying their best not to laugh.

At any rate, Lenny calmed down enough to accept my apology and agree that we were now even. Then, believe it or not, he continued to eat his damaged hot dogs and fries!

The rest of the day was pretty calm. Roz and Jan both kept as close to Sheldon as possible. Fran was having a ball with both Nicky and Norman to talk to. Lenny kept mostly to himself, alternating between speeding around the rink and buying more junk food to eat. I skated around from one group to another, never taking my eyes off Lenny the entire time. Even though he had called a truce, you never knew what he was capable of doing if I let my guard down!

I arrived home feeling good about everything. For one thing, we had proven that girls were just as good skaters as boys were. But more than that, the Gruesome Four had managed to successfully complete our first date with the older boys.

Before we split up to go home, Sheldon had mentioned going skating again sometime. And although the boys he had picked to come along this time were less than ideal, there were more where they came from. Next time Sheldon might just show up with some really great boyfriend material. Then who could predict what kind of great things might follow?

Chapter Three

THAT NIGHT, I lay in bed thinking of all the future possibilities that could arise from our ice skating date. Next time Sheldon would bring three boys who were really cute, and we would all pair off as we skated around. Ice skating would lead to dates to the movies and then parties every weekend, and—

My fantasies of how wonderful it would be if every one of the Gruesome Four had boyfriends went on and on. Unfortunately, while I was fantasizing, I was not getting any sleep. As a result, I had more trouble than usual getting up in time for school the next morning.

By the time I made it to the spot on the park wall where I met Jan each morning, we were too late for our usual bus. The bus we did make was borderline— if there was no traffic, we could just get there before the late bell, provided we ran the three blocks to school. If there was traffic, forget it.

This morning, there was plenty of traffic. I sat in my

seat nervously checking my watch. Jan and I had been late three times last week. The last thing we needed was to be late again.

It was mornings like this that I didn't appreciate the fact that I went to Huntington at all. Our school is way downtown in Manhattan, almost an hour's ride from Washington Heights. But that's not even the worst part about Huntington. The worst is that Huntington is a school that's only for girls.

Why do Jan and I put up with this and go there? Well, back in sixth grade all our friends took a special test to get into Huntington. Jan and I were the only ones who made it. Everyone made a big deal about this. You see, Huntington is one of the best schools in the city. It's supposed to be an honor to go there. Since my parents have instilled in me the importance of getting a good education practically from the moment I was born, I made the decision to go to Huntington instead of to my neighborhood junior high school, 515.

Educationally, I guess my decision was the right one. Huntington has some great teachers who really care. We get all these advanced courses to take and special projects to do like working at the Manhattan School for the Blind. But socially, going to Huntington presented lots of problems for me. It's much harder to get something going with boys when you don't go to school with them.

Today was one of those days when I doubted going to Huntington was worth it. Jan and I practically killed ourselves running from the bus stop. We burst into our room and slid into our seats just as the late bell finished ringing.

Ms. Bouton, our teacher for homeroom and English, looked at us and sighed. "Well, girls, you made it on time for a change. Good thing, too. Because I'm sure you wouldn't have wanted to miss the announcement I have to make this morning."

Jan and I looked at each other in surprise. We had no idea what Ms. Bouton could say that might be so important. So we just settled down to listen.

"As those of you girls who were here early enough to have time to look at the eighth grade bulletin board already know," she began, throwing a meaningful look at Jan and me. "Huntington is instituting a new policy for eighth graders. It's to help you get on the right track toward what we would like to see you get out of your school career."

"School career?" I whispered to Jan. "She thinks school is a *career?*" Jan giggled, then slapped her hand over her mouth as Ms. Bouton once again looked our way.

"Next year, you'll be entering the senior high division of Huntington," Ms. Bouton continued. "There will be girls from other schools entering at that level, and the competition will become even more intense than it is now."

Even more intense. That was hard to imagine. All the girls at Huntington had been top students in their elementary schools all over the city. But it was a lot harder to be tops at Huntington where everyone was as smart as you were. Competition was absolutely fierce!

"To prepare you for what lies ahead of you," Ms. Bouton's voice broke into my thoughts, "we've added a little extra incentive. For those of you in the top ten percent of your class at the end of this year—that will be the top two girls in each of the five eighth grade classes—there will be a special recognition at our final assembly. You'll be called up to the stage and honored in front of your classmates and your parents. Not only that, you'll have first choice at picking your classes for your ninth grade program."

"First choice at picking classes!" Jan whispered to me excitedly. "That would be fantastic!"

I nodded my agreement. For all the best classes at Huntington get filled up fast. Getting to pick before everyone else in the grade was definitely an advantage I wanted to have.

"But you have to do better than just be in the top ten percent academically,'' Ms. Bouton added. "We're going to be considering your other attributes as well. Things like whether you participate in clubs, class events, and community service projects. You have to have at least a full year's service on your record in order to qualify. This is the way the colleges will be evaluating you someday, so you might as well get on the right track now."

Ms. Bouton waved some papers in the air. "Right here is a list of the clubs and extra-curricular activities available at Huntington. I know most of you already signed up for some activities when school started.

This is a second opportunity for you to choose to broaden your horizons. Look over the list and write down by your name the clubs you belong to and any additional activities you'd like to participate in this year. I'll pass the list around so you can sign up while I take attendance."

Ms. Bouton handed the list to the first girl in the semicircular row of desks in which we sat. She took her time reading it before signing it and passing it down the line.

While waiting for the list to come to me, I thought carefully about my situation. The only club I belonged to was the service club through which I helped out at the Manhattan School for the Blind. That usually took up two afternoons a week. I knew I should sign up for something additional, but I really didn't want to commit myself to so much time.

"What are you going to sign up for, Linda?" Jan asked when she got the list.

"Well, the service club, of course," I said. "I'm not sure about anything else."

"How about the art club? I belong to that. You were sorry you didn't join with me last year."

"I know," I admitted. "I do love art and all that. But I still want to leave some afternoons free after school to work on getting somewhere with the boys in the neighborhood."

"No boys are going to like you no matter what you do, Linda Berman," a fresh voice announced. "So you'd better sign up for all the clubs you can if you want to have a shot at the top ten!" It was Samantha

21

Milken, standing by my desk and leering at me, who uttered these words.

Samantha has to be my least favorite person at Huntington. Not only is she a weirdo—a throwback to the middle ages, always reading about knights and ladies and picturing herself as some sort of medieval princess—but she's stuck-up and snotty and thinks she knows everything. Samantha thinks she's a leader and tries to get the other girls in the class to do whatever she says. I don't go along with this at all. So Samantha and I didn't hit it off right from the beginning.

"Why don't you just float off somewhere and mind your own business, Samantha?" I replied. "I can choose my clubs for myself!"

A triumphant smirk crossed her face. Samantha loved it when she saw her remarks got to me. "Don't be so touchy, Linda; I was just trying to be helpful," she said with feigned innocence. "Because I'm sure you think you've got a shot at making it to the top ten. But I have news for you. You might have a high average, but socially you're way behind here at Huntington. Just look at how many clubs I've signed up for!"

I looked where she was pointing. Next to her name she had a club listed for every day of the week. She also had herself down for the Christmas and Easter party committees. Not to mention that she was a candidate for class president. And I knew Samantha always got good grades. With a social record like that, she would really be hard to beat.

I felt this clutching feeling in the pit of my stomach. I really did want to be in the top ten. If I only signed up for the service club, I would have nothing to fall back on if anything went wrong. I knew I should sign up for an additional club, just to be sure.

But that would give Samantha the satisfaction of my admitting she was a threat to me. There was no way I was going to do that.

"Maybe you need all those clubs to get into the top ten, Samantha, but I don't," I said with more confidence than I felt. Then I made a big show out of putting my name down for the service club and nothing else.

For a moment, I actually thought I had scored one on Samantha. But when I saw her looking my way and giggling with one of her stuck-up followers, I realized the dumb thing I had done. Samantha had set me up, and I had played right into her hands.

Because I had signed up for just one club, I had put myself in the position where I would have to make it through the year with the service club no matter what. If anything went wrong I would wind up disqualifying myself from the top ten.

I quickly put the thought out of my mind by telling myself that nothing would go wrong. I would manage to show up Samantha one way or another.

After all, school wasn't the only important thing in my life. There had to be a balance. Now that the Gruesome Four had gotten the momentum going with the older boys, I had to have some time to work on really getting things rolling!

Chapter Four

DESPITE MY COMMITMENT to getting something going with the older boys, nothing new developed until the following Sunday. And even that day started out to be a big disappointment. It was raining—not a day for ice skating at all. The Gruesome Four sat miserably on the staircase in the hallway of my apartment building, not knowing what to do with ourselves.

My hallway was the place we often went to hang out when there was nowhere else to go. That was because my building was centrally located in the middle of Roz's, Fran's, and Jan's, and because there was a candy store right on my corner in case we got hungry.

Of course we could hang out inside my apartment if we wanted to. But my apartment is small. There are only two bedrooms—one for my parents and one shared by my brothers, Ira and Joey, who are twins and can be very bratty. I sleep in the living room so there's no privacy for us in my apartment at all. And today we were talking about private stuff. Like how we need to find a few eligible older boys.

Just when we were running out of ideas and things looked bleakest, I came up with this brainstorm. We would go bowling. There were always all sorts of boys at the bowling alley on a rainy day.

Unfortunately, half the other kids in the neighborhood must have had the same idea. The bowling alley was jammed, and we had to wait for ages until a lane opened up for us.

But the lane we finally got was well worth waiting for. There, bowling in the lane right next to us, were three teenage boys.

"They look pretty good from a distance," said Fran, squinting through her glasses as we approached the lane.

"Well, don't stare at them or anything," I said. "We don't want to look too obvious. Just pretend they don't interest us at all."

We purposely avoided looking at the boys as we sat down and put on our bowling shoes. I got up to bowl first.

I was very conscious of the fact that the boys might be watching me. I grabbed my bowling ball and took careful aim. Then I swayed up to the foul line, trying to make my approach look as sexy as possible in the hope that the boys might notice me.

They noticed me all right. Somehow, my finger got stuck in the ball, and I dropped it with a loud bang. Even worse, the ball landed in their lane, interrupting their game. Feeling like a complete fool, I ran after the ball and picked it up.

The boys all started laughing. I stood there, holding the ball and wishing I could disappear. Then I turned around to face them. "Just what's so funny, anyhow?" I demanded angrily.

"Well, if you want to know the truth, Linda. You're supposed to throw the ball down your own lane!" one of the boys answered. He smiled at me and came closer.

How did he know my name? I looked at him carefully for the first time. Why, it was Danny Kopler! I couldn't believe it!

Danny lived in the apartment right above mine. When we were little, we used to play together all the time. In fact, when I was four and Danny was six, we were boyfriend and girlfriend in a baby sort of way. Once we got older, we went our separate ways. Even though we lived in the same building, I hadn't talked to Danny for almost a year.

Boy, had he changed! He had gotten taller and chubbier. His voice was much deeper. You could see little short hairs on his face where he was already shaving. Danny was really starting to grow up. No wonder I hadn't recognized him right away!

It was just too bad we had to rediscover one another under these circumstances. I was so embarrassed. I could feel my face flushing.

"Uh, hi, Danny," I gulped. "What are you doing here?"

"Bowling, of course," he answered. "I'm here with

my friends." He pointed to the two boys sitting on the bench. "This is Linda Berman, guys. And those two clowns are Marty Amstell and Louie Fields."

Marty did kind of look like a clown. He was short and wore glasses. He had pale sickly skin with a scattering of pimples. But Louie was something else.

He was gorgeous! He had dirty blond hair that needed to be cut. It made him look lovable, like a sheepdog. His eyes were a beautiful blue, and they crinkled when he smiled at me. One look at him and it was as if none of the other boys I had ever liked before mattered at all.

For a moment I stood there just staring at Louie. He was wearing a soft-looking brown sweater. I could picture myself encircled by that sweater, just sinking into his arms.

"Aren't you going to introduce us to your friends, Linda?" Danny's voice shattered my delicious daydream.

"Huh?" I looked around and saw that the rest of the Gruesome Four, whom I had completely forgotten, were standing there waiting for me. "Oh, sure. That's Fran Zaro, Roz Buttons, and Jan Zieglebaum," I introduced. "We just decided to take up bowling. You know, good exercise and all that." I tried to sound cool.

"Well, we're just about finishing our games," said Danny. "But we could hang around and give you girls some pointers, if you like."

I looked at my friends. Roz and Jan didn't look enthused. They were both so stuck on Sheldon that no one else mattered. But Fran was nodding her frizzy head joyfully. "Sure, I guess we could benefit from some expert skill," I answered happily.

If I had known how badly I would bowl, I would have thought twice before saying yes to the boys. It really was humiliating!

While Marty kept score, Danny and Louie showed us how to take the right approach and how to release the ball properly. But the more I concentrated on their advice, the worse I bowled.

I knew it was Louie's presence that was causing the problem. I got so nervous every time he came close to me that I could hardly breathe, must less aim a bowling ball.

But it turned out to be worth the humiliation. The boys waited until we had finished bowling, and then we wound up walking home together. On the way, I found out a lot more about Louie. He, Danny, and Marty had been in the same class in junior high, but now they went to different high schools. Danny and Marty went to Stuyvesant. Louie went to the Bronx High School of Technology. Like Huntington, both schools were special schools that you had to take a test to get into.

Their friendship was cemented by a common interest in math, of all things. Danny was a mathematical genius. He had even taught himself calculus. Louie and Marty both wanted to go into computers.

As we walked, I stood next to Danny. But as I listened to him talk, I kept looking past him. I couldn't keep my eyes off Louie. His skin was so smooth; his eyes were so sparkling, and his hair shone with glints of gold.

It took me a while, but I finally got up the courage to talk to him directly. "So you go to Bronx Tech, Louie. How do you like it there?"

He shrugged. "It's not bad—for a school. There are some really good teachers there—especially if you're interested in math and computers like I am."

"Really? That's great. Math and computers always fascinated me!" I said enthusiastically.

"But Linda," Jan began. "You never liked—oof!"

Sometimes Jan has no sense. I had to shove my elbow into her ribs to keep her from telling Louie that I never liked math and computers very much. After all, it wasn't that I didn't like math. It was just that I liked other subjects more. Like art and English and social studies and science. But math was starting to look a lot better to me all of a sudden. So was the idea which Louie had just given me—of changing schools myself and going to Bronx Technology.

"As a matter of fact, I've been thinking about taking the test for Bronx Tech this year," I announced. "I've been getting kind of tired of going to school with only girls. Tech would be a perfect change of pace." I looked at Louie when I said that, hoping for a positive reaction to my words.

But before he could say anything, Jan piped up again. "You mean you would leave me all alone at Huntington and go off to Bronx Technology by yourself, Linda?"

"Of course not." I couldn't believe it. For a moment

I had been so dazzled by Louie that I let myself forget completely about Jan. But the answer to the problem was simple. "You can take the test for Bronx Tech, too, Jan. We can go there together. I'm sure we'll both like it better than Huntington. Don't you think so, Louie?"

"Me?" He looked at me strangely for a moment. Then he grinned this beautiful grin that caused my heart to positively pound. "Sure! Why not?" he said agreeably.

That was all it took. I was smitten. From that moment on I was madly, wildly, and completely blindly, crazy over Louie!

Why must parents be so difficult?

Bronx Technology is a good school. Every bit as good as Huntington. So I didn't think my parents would put up any opposition to my changing schools.

No such luck. My parents are so old-fashioned they seem like they're from another era. Education is the only thing that matters to them. "Forget changing schools," my father said flatly. "You stay at Huntington where you can concentrate on your school work. Education and boys don't mix!"

My eyes stung with tears of frustration. How could my parents treat me like a baby who didn't care about my education? I always worked hard and got good grades, but that didn't seem to matter to them. It just wasn't fair!

I turned to leave the room in defeat. Then I decided to make one last attempt by trying an approach I knew my parents could relate to. "Please," I begged. "Just let me take the test for Tech. We can decide later whether or not I should go. Right now I need the test-taking practice. For my future—when I take the college board tests."

That was the right thing to say. The college boards are way up there in importance to my parents. My mother looked at my father and he shrugged helplessly. "If it means that much to you," he mumbled.

I threw my arms around him and hugged him. "It does! It really does! Oh, Daddy! Thank you!"

Jan had even more trouble with her parents. Talk about old-fashioned. Her parents make mine seem practically modern. They would love to keep Jan a baby forever!

But once my parents gave in there was hope for Jan. She played it cool, crying to her parents about how awful it would be to have to travel all by herself once I went to Tech. The idea frightened her parents so much they agreed to let Jan take the test.

So Jan and I went together to take the test for Bronx Technology. We were very impressed. The school was in a new, modern building, not an old crumbling one like Huntington. The trip to Tech was shorter, too. But the best part was being in a school with boys once again. And walking down the hallways knowing that Louie could appear at any moment.

If I went to Bronx Technology, I could see Louie in the halls every day. I could ride to school with him on the subway. I might even eat lunch with him in the cafeteria. He would carry my books and put his arm around me and . . .

I was getting carried away. I forced my mind back to the test I was taking. After all, my dreams would amount to nothing if I didn't pass the test!

The test was hard. It was even harder than the test for Huntington had been. Jan thought so, too.

But we tried hard not to be discouraged. After all, we had found the test for Huntington to be hard when we took it, and we had passed, anyhow. We just had to hope that we would make Bronx Technology, too.

Chapter Five

JUST IN CASE we didn't make Bronx Tech, Jan and I still tried our hardest to keep in the running for the top ten at Huntington. We went to every meeting of the service club. Our assignment, to help with the Creative Arts Club at the Manhattan School, was fun because it was all artwork, but it still took a lot of our time.

Then there were midterm exams. Jan and I spent hours studying and testing each other on class material. Our grades were good, but Samantha Milken's were, too. We couldn't let up for a moment.

Once midterms were over, we were able to turn our attention to the area which had been sadly neglected—making some progress with the boys. We decided the best approach was to throw a party—at my house.

Arranging this was no easy task. I wanted to use my brothers' room for the party because it had a door that closed in case we were able to get some kissing games started. In order to get Ira and Joey to agree to this I had to bribe them by offering to take over their much-hated chore of taking out the garbage for an entire month. I had to go along with all sorts of silly rules from my parents—like no sitting on beds and no turning off lights. But, finally, we had a place for the party.

The next problem was developing a guest list of boys. Sheldon and Norman were definites, but they weren't enough to make a successful party. Fran and I wanted Danny and Louie to come, but we were afraid to ask them in case they said no. We would up taking the easy way out, once again asking Sheldon to bring some extra boys.

"Make sure they're nice ones this time," I told him. "No one like that horrid Lenny Lipoff!"

Sheldon promised he and Norman would show up with two nice boys. So the guest list was taken care of.

As we got closer to the party, it was eating me up inside that I was too chicken to ask Danny and Louie. I knew we would never get anywhere with them if we didn't try.

So one afternoon I worked up enough courage to arrange to "accidentally" run into Danny in the hall at the very time I knew he was due home from school. Then I casually mentioned that we were having a party with Sheldon and Norman and that he and Louie were welcome to drop by if they had nothing to do. My heart beat wildly as I waited for his response.

To my great joy, it was favorable. Danny didn't

make any promises, but he did say he would ask Louie if he wanted to come down for a while. So at least I had hope that Louie might come to the party.

I didn't think it was possible to be as nervous as I was before the party. It was as if there were butterflies having a party of their own in my stomach.

This was a big night for the Gruesome Four. It was our first attempt at a party with older boys. I wanted everything to be perfect, but everything started out all wrong.

For one thing, the two extra boys Sheldon brought were the same boys who had come to the ice skating rink—Nicky James and Lenny Lipoff.

I really didn't mind having Nicky. But Lenny Lipoff! I thought I had made it clear to Sheldon that I wanted no part of that troublemaker. I took Sheldon aside to a corner of the room and let him have it.

"Sheldon!" I whispered through clenched teeth. "How could you bring Lenny here when you know how I feel about him? He's nothing but trouble!"

Sheldon just laughed. "That's not true, Linda. Lenny's got to be the funniest person I know."

"Well, I'm not interested in his kind of fun. I want you to get him out of here before he does something crazy!"

"I can't do that. I invited him. Look, Linda, since Lenny's already here, why don't you give him a chance? He can be really nice when you get to know him. I promise to keep him in line."

I looked over at Lenny. He was helping himself to

big handfuls of potato chips and pretzels and looking perfectly innocent, even cute. Maybe, with Sheldon to control him, it would be possible for Lenny to behave himself at the party.

"Okay, Sheldon. Lenny can stay," I decided. "But remember. This is a personal favor to you. I expect you to keep Lenny from making trouble."

"I will, I will," Sheldon promised with a grin.

Despite Sheldon's promise, it didn't take long before Lenny started getting into things. He stood in the center of the room with a bowl of M & M candies and began flipping them into the air. He opened his mouth wide and tried to catch the M & M's in it.

He wasn't very successful. M & M's bounced off his face and rolled all over the floor.

"Cut that out, Lenny!" I yelled. "You're getting M & M's all over! We don't want roaches in here!"

"Too late for that now," he shouted. "There's a roach flying at you right now!"

A brown thing landed in my lap. "Yuck!" I shrieked and brushed it away. The thing bounced across my brother's bed.

It was only a chocolate M & M. The boys all laughed and started throwing the rest of the M & M's at us girls. They were having lots of fun, but I wasn't. If my parents came in and saw what was going on it would be the end of the party!

The ringing of the doorbell saved everything. The boys all settled down and even helped pick up the candies. I went to the door. "Who's there?" I asked.

"Police!" a deep voice answered. "You'd better keep the noise down in there! Open up, now!"

Frightened, I opened the door a crack. There were no police in the hall. It was Danny and Louie!

My heart pounded with joy as I opened the door for them.

"We're crashing this party," Danny announced. "It's time to put a little life into it!"

Danny seemed to know just what our party needed. He suggested playing a game called Rome, London, and Paris.

This turned out to be a new kissing game. The beauty of it was that you played it while dancing. That way, if my mother came in, it wouldn't look bad at all.

One person worked the lights. That was Norman because he had no interest in kissing games. When he called "Rome," everyone would change partners. When he called "London," you would hold your partner close. When he called "Paris," he would shut off the lights and you were supposed to kiss your partner.

I couldn't wait. Maybe I would wind up with Louie! He was wearing that same soft sweater he wore that day in the bowling alley. I closed my eyes and imagined his arms around me, the touch of his lips on mine.

"Shall we start, Linda?" My eyes flew open. It was Danny, asking me to dance. He had a strange look on his face.

"Okay." I followed him onto the dancing area. He held me tightly even before Norman called "London." I felt very uncomfortable.

"Rome," Norman called out. That meant we changed partners. I breathed more easily as Danny let me go. "We'll do 'Paris' next time," he whispered to me.

I wound up with Sheldon next. Since he was only a few inches taller than I, he was very easy to dance with. I relaxed in his arms and thought about Danny. Why was he looking at me like that tonight? Could it be that Danny liked me as a girlfriend? Didn't he realize that I was crazy about Louie?

"Paris," Norman called out. Thinking of Danny, I hardly felt Sheldon kiss me softly on the lips. I opened my eyes and looked around the room. Fran and Danny were still kissing. They looked as if they were really enjoying themselves. Where was Louie? My heart sank as I saw him with his arms around Roz.

"Rome!" I tried moving closer to Louie, hoping he'd get the hint and ask me to dance. But somehow he wound up with Fran and I with Lenny.

"I see you've really got a thing for Louie," Lenny commented.

"How did you know?" I asked, horrified. "Was I that obvious?"

"Don't worry," he whispered. "I'll take care of things for you."

"Rome!" Lenny left me and went to the corner to talk to Louie. There was a cover on the radiator that we used as a window seat. They sat there, deep in conversation, occasionally glancing at me. I was dying. What could Lenny be saying to him?

I saw Danny heading in my direction. I looked

around frantically for an escape. There was none. I found myself clasped in Danny's arms again.

"I missed you," he whispered.

"Oh," I replied, not knowing what to say. I was beginning to feel those butterflies in my stomach again.

"Paris!" I saw Danny's mouth headed toward mine. Quickly, I turned my head to the side. His kiss landed on my cheek.

I couldn't take it anymore. I decided it was time to refill the punchbowl. Fran was near me. I grabbed her arm and pulled her out the door and into the kitchen.

"Hey! Where are we going?" she complained. "This party was just starting to be fun!"

"Look, Fran. I've got to talk to you!" I furiously poured in the punch. "It's about Danny."

"Danny," she repeated dreamily. "He's so comfortable to dance with. And he kisses so sweetly!"

"Sweetly? Danny?" I looked at Fran with amazement. "Fran! Are you starting to fall for Danny?"

'I guess so," she admitted. "I know he's not good looking, but there's something about him I really like. He's so intelligent. And when I'm with him, it just feels right!"

"Why—uh—that's great, Fran!" My head was spinning. Now how was I going to tell her that I was afraid that Danny liked me?

"What was it you wanted to tell me about Danny, Linda?"

"Oh—uh—nothing, really. Just that the two of you looked so good dancing together!" Anxious to end this conversation, I picked up the bowl of punch. "Let's bring this back to the party!"

Lenny asked me to dance as soon as I got back to the room. He had a mischievous grin plastered all over his face.

"Okay, Lenny. What are you up to now?"

"Who me? What makes you think I'm up to something?" he asked innocently.

"Aren't you always?"

"Don't be paranoid, Linda!"

"Paranoid? What do you mean?"

"You know. Thinking someone's always plotting against you," he laughed. Just as I started to relax, I saw him wink and gesture to Louie. I was furious!

"If you told Louie I like him, I'll never speak to you again, big mouth Lenny," I fumed. But Lenny just threw back his head and laughed his maddening laugh.

"Rome!" Norman cried out, flipping the lights back on. I was so mad, I didn't even see Louie approaching.

"Dance, Linda?" he asked, softly.

I felt so weak that I didn't think my legs were going to hold me up. I collapsed in Louie's arms, feeling their strength. His sweater was just as soft as I had imagined it to be.

"London!" I felt Louie's arms tighten around me. My heart was beating rapidly. Now if only Norman would call "Paris."

"Paris!" Norman did it! The room darkened as he shut off the lights. My body tensed, waiting for Louie's kiss.

Then the lights flicked back on unexpectedly.

"Hey, why did you do that, Norman?" I heard Lenny call out. "I didn't even get a chance to kiss Fran." He stood with his arms around her, his face bent halfway down.

"There will be none of that in this house! I don't approve of this kind of party at all!" An angry voice came from the doorway. I looked in that direction and felt this pain grip my stomach. Louie's arms dropped from my shoulders.

It was my father who had put the lights back on. My father is usually very quiet. But when he gets mad, forget it! There's no arguing with him. And he really looked mad now, his bushy eyebrows drawn together in a frown.

"We weren't doing anything, Daddy," I tried to explain. "Just playing a game."

"Didn't your mother tell you to keep the lights on?"

"Well, er-yes!" I stammered. "But they weren't really off, either. I mean they were just being flicked off and right back on again. I mean—uh—it was just a game!"

"That's enough of these games, now," my father stated firmly. He looked at his watch. "Besides, it's almost ten o'clock. Time for this party to be over. Everyone can just go home now. You're not grown up yet, you know!"

"Ten o'clock!" I heard Lenny complain to Sheldon. "Who ever heard of a party's being over at ten o'clock! What kind of baby party did you drag me to, anyhow?"

I was positively humiliated. But I knew better than

to argue with my father. The boys got their coats and started filing out into the hall, grumbling to themselves.

The party was over. I was robbed of my chance to kiss Louie. Now the whole neighborhood would know that the Gruesome Four were too young to have a party past ten o'clock on a Saturday night!

Chapter Six

Despite the abrupt ending of our party, it did get things going with the older boys. The candy store on my corner became a hangout for all of us. Someone would always show up to talk to or fool around with. But real relationships, the kind we wanted with the boys, were slow to develop.

Unfortunately, there was one relationship between an older boy and me that was developing, but in a way I never intended it to. It started because I was trying to get some extra credit toward my standing in the top ten at Huntington. I volunteered to spend additional time at the Manhattan School before Christmas. Since there was so much to do helping the blind kids make holiday decorations, Jan and I wound up there almost every afternoon.

The president of the Manhattan School's Creative Arts Club was Jeremy Layne. Jeremy was sixteen and almost totally blind. He could see only lights and shadow and well-lit shapes, but he was really a terrific person.

For one thing, except for his eyes, which were clouded with a sort of opaque film, he was good looking. He was smart, able to keep up with all the work on his grade level by reading braille almost as fast as I could read print. Not only that, Jeremy was an artist. He created these beautiful modern art paintings with happy, sparkling colors.

When I had first met Jeremy, I couldn't believe those were actually his paintings that were hanging in the front lobby of the Manhattan School. I mean, how could a person who couldn't see create paintings that looked so good?

But by Christmas time, I had worked enough with Jeremy to realize he could do most anything. Then, one afternoon, we finished early with our group of kids, who were sticking decorations on paper Christmas trees. Jan decided to take the kids aside to read them a story while Jeremy and I cleaned up. When we were done, Jeremy totally surprised me by asking me if I'd like to watch him paint.

"I want you to know that it's not just everyone I let hang around when I'm painting," he said with a grin.

"I know, I know. I'm really flattered," I answered. And I was. Because I knew Jeremy well enough by then to realize he was shy around most sighted people.

We went into a small room off the main art room. It was there that Jeremy did his personal work.

I watched with amazement as he set up his colors. "I have every tube labeled in braille," he explained.

"I set up the colors in order—according to the rainbow. I know just where each color is so I don't have to fumble around for them."

"That makes sense," I said. "But how do you know where to put what color?"

"Well, the first thing I do is divide the canvas into smaller sections." He took out a ball of string and some tape. "I use pieces of string for that. Then it's easier to plan which color goes where."

I watched with amazement as Jeremy worked. He put on the paint with a palette knife, building up thick layers that he could feel with his sensitive fingers.

At first he talked to me, explaining what he was doing and the reason why he was choosing each color. Stuff like blue to represent cool calmness and yellow for sunshine and happiness. But then, as he became more involved in his painting, he stopped talking altogether. I sat and watched him in silence, feeling very close to him.

Suddenly, there was a knock on the door and Jan's voice filtered from the other side. "Linda? Are you in there? Do you know what time it is? We've got to start heading home."

I looked at my watch. It was hard to believe it was four-thirty already! Jan and I usually left by four. I had gotten so engrossed in watching Jeremy, I had completely forgotten about the time.

"I'll be right there, Jan." I got up from my chair. "Sorry I can't watch you finish painting, Jeremy. I've got to go."

Jeremy's hands stopped their busy movement. "Do

you really have to go, Linda? You're the inspiration for this painting, you know."

"I am?" I gave a nervous little laugh. "That's really sweet of you, Jeremy. But if Jan and I don't get moving right now, we're going to get stuck in the worst part of the rush hour." I opened the door and Jan handed me my coat.

"Oh. I forgot about the rush hour." He smiled. "Well, I guess this is the last time I'll see you till after vacation. That is—unless—unless you'd like to come back after school tomorrow to see the Christmas performance we're giving. We've got some great acts."

"Christmas performance?" I looked at Jan and she shrugged. "Well, I guess Jan and I could come to that. See you tomorrow, then, Jeremy." Before he could say anything else, Jan and I were out the door and heading toward the subway.

"You know, Linda. I don't think Jeremy meant to invite me to the show at all," Jan said as we waited on the platform. "I think he just wanted you to come."

"Just me? Why would you think that?"

"Because I think Jeremy likes you, Linda," Jan said with a giggle.

"Likes me? You mean as a girlfriend?"

Jan nodded and giggled again.

"Don't be silly, Jan. Jeremy and I are just good friends," I insisted.

But now that Jan mentioned it, there were times that he did act as if I was special. The thought made me really uncomfortable. Because I didn't want Jeremy to feel that way about me at all.

*　　*　　*

Jeremy had saved two seats for us next to him in the second row. "You go in first, Jan, and take the seat next to Jeremy," I whispered. I didn't think that what Jan said about Jeremy's liking me as a girlfriend was true, but, just in case, it would be safer to have her sitting between us.

But Jeremy didn't allow this to happen. When he heard Jan coming, he got up and told her to squeeze past him. This way, he wound up sitting in the middle. I gave Jan a panic-stricken look. But there was nothing she could do to change the seating arrangement without looking obvious.

"I'm glad you girls could come," said Jeremy. "This is supposed to be an especially good show. The kids will be acting out scenes from famous Christmas carols while the chorus sings."

"Sounds great!" I tried to sound enthusiastic. But once the show started, I began to relax and get into it. Because it really was good. The fact that most of the audience couldn't see hadn't kept the blind kids from going all out on the costumes and scenery. The singing was wonderful.

I, who couldn't sing a note without someone telling me to shut up, was totally caught up in the whole scene. I really forgot where I was. That is, until this romantic part of "Winter Wonderland," where the boy and girl are pretending the snowman is the person who's going to marry them. That was when I noticed that Jeremy's hand, which had been resting up against mine, had somehow closed in around my fingers. He

47

shifted slightly, and before I knew what was happening, he was sitting there holding my hand!

I froze. I mean I sat there as if I was petrified. I didn't dare move a muscle because I figured if I was to move my hand one way, Jeremy would interpret it as if I was encouraging him and I liked him. If I was to move it another way, he might think I was rejecting him.

I didn't want to hurt Jeremy's feelings, but I didn't want to encourage him either. Besides, maybe he didn't really mean anything by it. Maybe he was just holding my hand to be friendly.

Suddenly, it started getting very hot sitting there in the second row. The lights from the stage shone right on me, and I could feel the sweat beading up on my forehead. My armpits were sticky, and the palms of my hands, especially the one that Jeremy was holding, were soaking wet. How I wished I could be somewhere else—anywhere else.

"Winter Wonderland" finally ended. Everyone began clapping, which was the perfect excuse to get my hand away from Jeremy's. When I finished clapping, I wiped my sweating palms off on my skirt. Then I clasped my hands together and laid them in my lap as far away from Jeremy as possible.

The show ended without further incident. I said good-bye to Jeremy, thanked him for inviting Jan and me to the show, and told him I hoped he had a good vacation back home with his family. Then I grabbed Jan's hand and took off out of the Manhattan School as fast as I could.

"Hey, Linda, slow down! What's your hurry?" Jan asked as she struggled to keep up with me. I was far enough away from the school now to feel safe, so I stopped and told her about what had happened.

"See! I told you Jeremy liked you!" She giggled.

"Jan! It's not funny!" I said. "I've got to work with Jeremy on this club stuff for the rest of this school year. How am I going to handle it if he likes me?"

"You'll come up with something, Linda." Jan tried to stifle her giggles with only limited success. "You always do. Besides, it's vacation now. You don't have to even think of Jeremy or anything related to Huntington until the new year!"

"True." I brightened. "I can devote all my time this vacation to getting somewhere with Louie!"

It took a while, but toward the end of Christmas vacation, Fran and I finally made some real progress. We got an invitation to spend an evening with Danny and Louie!

It seems that Danny has this collection of *Mad* magazines dating back to practically the first edition. Fran and I told him that there could be nothing more fascinating than sitting around looking through old issues of *Mad*. So Danny invited us to come up that night and check out his collection. Louie was going to be there, too.

Unfortunately, I wound up setting myself up for another awkward situation. I was so anxious to see Louie that I made the mistake of arriving at Danny's before anyone else did.

Danny's mother let me in and then busied herself in the kitchen. Danny was in his room sitting on his bed, his *Mad* magazines arranged in stacks around him, when I walked in. His eyes lit up when he saw me. He moved some stacks of magazines to the floor and patted the bed next to him. "Sit right here, Linda!"

Frantically, I looked around the room, but I was trapped. The only places to sit, other than the bed, were a piano bench and a desk chair across the room. It would look silly for me to sit way over there. So I sat down on the corner of the bed. I grabbed a magazine and began leafing through it.

Danny made it impossible for me to concentrate. He stretched out close to me. He rested his head on his hand and stared up adoringly at my face.

I squirmed. I pretended not to notice him. But it was extremely uncomfortable having Danny so close to me. I bet my profile looked awful from so close. I bet my nose looked huge! I could feel a pimple developing on my chin. Was he staring at the pimple?

I shifted my position. I brought my hand up to my face and cupped my chin in my palm. By extending my fingers, I covered most of my face.

It didn't help much. From the corner of my eye, I could see Danny's face come even closer to mine. I moved to the very edge of the bed.

"Linda?" I heard him take a deep breath.

I slowly turned toward him. He was so close that I could see where his forehead was all broken out. That and the sheepish expression on his face made my stomach turn. It growled loudly.

"Yes, Danny?" I forced myself to look at him.

"Do you remember when we met in the bowling alley after not seeing each other for so long?"

"Of course."

"Well, I knew then that the renewal of our relationship was a momentous occasion—the start of a whole new direction for both of us."

"W-what do you mean, Danny?" I asked uncomfortably.

"Do you remember how we were almost like brother and sister when we were kids? How we were so affectionate with one another?"

"Y-yes."

"Well—it's not like that for me anymore! I mean, the affection is still there, but it's no longer brotherly!" As he said this, Danny stared directly into my eyes.

I couldn't take it! The little problem with Jeremy was nothing compared to this. I mean, Danny was really coming on to me. How could I explain how I felt without hurting his feelings? To make matters worse, Fran would be heartbroken when she found out that Danny liked me. Fran! But maybe that was the answer. Fran was my perfect excuse—she would soften the blow!

"Stop, D-Danny," I stammered. "We have to think about Fran!"

"Fran?" He leaned still closer.

"Yes, Fran!" I jumped off the bed and backed away from him. "Fran is one of my best friends. And she's crazy about you, Danny—ever since that night at my party."

"She is?" He looked confused.

I took a step back toward him. "Now don't ever let her know that I told you this, Danny. But it would just break Fran's heart if anything happened between you and me. I want you to know that you'll always be special to me. But it will just have to be in a brother-sister sort of way. For Fran's sake."

I could see that Danny was digesting this information and deciding what to do. So, just to make sure he understood exactly where things stood, I added the clincher.

"Besides, Danny," I said. "I'm crazy about Louie. I'll always be grateful to you for introducing me to him."

"Oh." Danny's face dropped. But then he perked up again. "Well, I guess if you look at this scientifically, it really is an interesting development. Fran likes me; I like you; you like Louie. And Louie—well, we don't know about Louie, do we? Too bad we can't solve this like a mathematical equation!"

He laughed and patted the bed again. "Why don't you sit back down while we're waiting for the rest of this foursome. Maybe we can straighten this out by working on changing your mind!"

He grabbed my hand, and I felt all panicky again. Just as I was about to bolt and run, I was saved by the ringing of the doorbell. Danny got up to answer it. It was Fran and Louie, arriving at the same time. Fran gave me a questioning look when she saw me alone there with Danny. I just shrugged my shoulders and smiled weakly.

We had a great time that night at Danny's. I tried to stay as far away from him as possible, but it wasn't even necessary. Knowing that Fran liked him seemed to make a big difference to Danny. He kept looking at her and paying attention to her all evening.

That left me free to concentrate on Louie. I did what all those advice-to-teenagers columns tell you to do. I kept him talking about himself. He told me all about Bronx Technology and his math and his bowling. I found out that he has a little brother just five years old.

I was starting to feel really close to Louie. The closer I felt, the more I liked him. If only he would feel that way about me, too.

The evening was cut short because Fran had to be home at 9:00. Her parents are even stricter than mine. Because we were at Danny's, I was allowed out until 10:00, so we decided we would all walk Fran home.

Fran's house is four blocks from my house. To get there you have to walk up Broadway, a street bustling with traffic and stores. The stores were lit with Christmas decorations, and a holiday feeling was in the air. The temperature had dropped, and I could see my breath frosting in the darkness. Listening to Fran's chatter, I walked between Danny and Louie. I was silent, but happy. It had been a wonderful evening.

New Year's Eve was a night the Gruesome Four all looked forward to. Unfortunately, we weren't able to get a party together with the boys, but we did get Fran to convince her parents to let us sleep over at her house. Sleepovers were always a lot of fun.

When I arrived at Fran's, Roz was already there. Fran and I were filling her in on the details of our evening with Danny and Louie, when the telephone rang.

Fran answered it. When she came back into the room, her face was absolutely white. "That was Jan," she announced, sinking down on her bed. "She's not coming."

"Not coming?" Roz and I said together. "But why?"

"You're not going to believe this," Fran shook her frizzy head. "Do you remember the other night when Danny, Louie, and you walked me home, Linda?"

"Sure. But what does that have to do with Jan?" I asked.

"It seems some friend of Jan's mother saw us together."

"So? I still don't know what that has to do with Jan."

"Logically, it should have nothing to do with Jan. But this busybody knows we're all friends. She told Mrs. Zieglebaum she shouldn't allow Jan to hang around with us because we do terrible things like holding hands in the street with boys!"

I sprang up from where I had been sitting on the bed. "What are you talking about, Fran? Terrible things like holding hands? That's ridiculous! Besides, no one was holding hands in the first place."

"Well, as a matter of fact, I was," Fran admitted. "Danny held my hand for two whole blocks."

"He did? I didn't see you holding hands!" I said in amazement.

"I know." Fran smiled sheepishly. "I was going to tell you about it tonight. It was going to be a New Year's Eve surprise—kind of a symbol that the Gruesome Four was finally getting someplace."

"Why that's wonderful, Fran!" I said. "Or at least it would be if it wasn't for that busybody's making trouble!"

Fran took off her glasses and her eyes sparked angrily. "What makes me mad is that Mrs. Zieglebaum could let something dumb like that be a reason to keep us away from Jan. After we've been friends for so long, too!"

"It's awful, that's what it is," said Roz. "And it's just not fair!"

"Fair or not fair, I bet Mrs. Zieglebaum is doing this on purpose," I said grimly. "And you know what? I think she's been waiting for an opportunity to do something like this for a while now."

"What do you mean, Linda?" asked Fran.

"I mean I think Mrs. Zieglebaum has been very unhappy about the fact that we're starting to do things with older boys. She thinks Jan is too young for that kind of stuff. So she doesn't really want Jan to be friends with us at all!"

"Don't be silly, Linda," said Roz. "Mrs. Zieglebaum is friendly with my mother and with Fran's.

She's the one who wanted us all to be friends in the first place.''

"True," I admitted. "But that was before we were interested in older boys. I hope I'm wrong. But I just have this awful feeling that Mrs. Zieglebaum is going to come up with one excuse after another to keep Jan out of the Gruesome Four!''

Chapter Seven

MRS. ZIEGLEBAUM MIGHT have been able to keep Jan away from us on New Year's Eve, but once school started, I was back to seeing her every day again. Jan acted like nothing had happened, so I decided to hope that my theory about Mrs. Zieglebaum was wrong, and to wait and see what developed.

Besides, I had enough to worry about at Huntington. Like how I was going to go back to the Manhattan School and face Jeremy.

I saw now how big a mistake it was to have signed up for just one club. With the service club as my only extra-curricular activity, I had no choice but to stick with it. If I quit, I would be out of the running for the top ten eighth graders. I wasn't going to let that happen—not after I had put in so much work to keep my grades high.

Besides, I really liked working with the blind kids at the Manhattan School. And I certainly enjoyed doing art. Actually, I enjoyed Jeremy, too—before he complicated everything by acting as if he liked me as a girlfriend.

To make matters worse, Jan was absent the day of our first club meeting. That meant I had to face Jeremy on my own. I decided to meet the problem head on. With a little luck, maybe Jeremy had forgotten he liked me over the vacation. Maybe he had quit the Creative Arts Club. Maybe there was a way I could avoid him altogether.

He was sitting near the door to the art room when I arrived that afternoon. He was busy showing some little kids how to cut something out of folded pieces of paper.

I thought quickly. Maybe I could just tiptoe around to the other side of the room and start working with someone over there. If I was quiet enough, maybe Jeremy wouldn't even notice that I was there. Then I would just say a quick "hi" and "good-bye" to him, right before it was time to leave.

It didn't work. Jeremy's senses are almost uncanny. Even though I tried my best to be quiet, he must have recognized my footsteps or something. Because he called out, "Hi, Linda! Come see what we're doing here!"

Well, I certainly didn't want to be rude to him. Reluctantly, I walked over to his table.

"What are you making?" I asked. But, all the while, my mind was struggling to think up an excuse to get away from him as soon as possible.

"Snowflake pictures," he said. "First you cut the

white paper into a six-sided shape. Then you fold it up and cut out little designs. When you open it again, you get a lacy pattern like a snowflake.'' He unfolded the paper he was working on so I could see what he had done. ''You make all different sizes, then paste them on a black background to get a really dramatic picture.''

''Hey that looks great!'' I admired a finished work. ''Let me try that!'' Forgetting my whole plot to keep as far from Jeremy as possible, I sat down across from him and began helping a partially sighted seven-year-old cut the paper correctly. Maybe I was better off just acting natural and pretending nothing was different with Jeremy.

I kept my hands busy cutting so Jeremy couldn't get near them. I tried to stick to safe topics of conversation, like what he did when he was home for Christmas vacation. The only problem came when he asked me about what I had done on my vacation.

''Well—I—er—'' I stammered. For what could I tell him? That the whole focus of my vacation had been to work on getting closer to Louie, the boy I was crazy about? If Jeremy liked me, that would be the last thing he wanted to hear.

So I just told him about the whole group in general— the Gruesome Four, gawky Nicky, loudmouth Lenny, handsome Sheldon and Louie, and Danny, the genius. I told him how Roz and Fran were finally getting closer to the boys they liked and how Jan's mother thought it was all just terrible.

Jeremy listened to me intently the whole time. He

laughed at the funny parts of my story and was really sympathetic about what happened with Jan.

I could tell from watching his expression that his feelings hadn't changed. He still liked me. I did like him, too—as a friend.

Jeremy was so nice that it made me feel worse than ever that I couldn't like him as a boyfriend. I just hoped that nothing further would come up along those lines so I would never have to hurt his feelings.

A new bowling alley opened up in our neighborhood for the new year. Danny, Louie, and Marty decided to form a team that bowled every Saturday morning. Much to my surprise, Danny and Louie stopped by my house one Saturday and asked me to come along with them.

"Our team needs a lucky charm," said Danny with a grin. "And we've decided you're it, Linda!"

"Me? You want me to be your lucky charm?"

"Sure! Why not?" said Louie.

"Well, what do I have to do?"

"Not much. Just come with us whenever we bowl and root for us. That'll bring us good luck," Danny explained.

"Well, okay. I don't have much else to do on Saturday mornings, anyhow," I said. I quickly calculated that I'd have to get up an hour earlier in order to get the vacuuming and my other chores done in time to go with them to the bowling alley. But what was a little sleep to sacrifice for the opportunity to be lucky charm for Danny and Louie?

When we arrived at the alleys, Marty had already found their assigned lane. "Hi, Marty!" I sang out. "Guess who's going to be your lucky charm?" But my joyful mood was immediately shattered when I noticed that Marty had someone with him.

It was a girl. A girl I'd seen before. A girl I didn't like, even though I had never spoken to her.

She had to be the bustiest girl in the whole neighborhood, and she obviously wasn't trying to hide the fact. She wore a tight T-shirt and tighter pants. She had on tons of make-up—red lipstick, black eyeliner, and bright green eyeshadow.

Marty introduced her to everyone. "This is Renee Berkley. We've been going out together recently."

Going out with Marty! I looked at Renee with increasing admiration. I knew Renee was the same age I was, but she had an older boy for a boyfriend—even if it was only Marty. Renee had achieved success!

I decided to watch every move she made. Maybe I could pick up some hints on the way mature girls should act.

That morning, I spent more time observing Renee than I did watching the boys bowl. What I saw made me feel sick. I could never act like Renee did. She was totally open about flirting with the boys. She went right up to them, batting her mascara-covered eyelashes and gazing into their faces.

She talked incessantly in a high-pitched voice. Whenever one of the boys made a comment, she giggled as if it was the funniest thing ever said.

When we first arrived, she hovered around Marty.

At time went on, I noticed her spending more and more time with Louie!

She flitted around him, applauding whenever he made a strike. "Great shot, Louie! What an arm you have, Louie! You're really some fantastic bowler, Louie!"

You would think that Louie was her boyfriend and not Marty. Marty kept on bowling and didn't even seem to care. But I did! I felt this cloud of gloom settling all around me. I grew quiet and sat stiffly on the bench, my chin cupped in my hand.

Louie was in his glory. He bowled his highest score, ever. Every game was over two hundred.

"Oh, Louie! You're wonderful!" Renee gushed in her squeaky voice. "I think I'll come here every Saturday just to see you bowl!"

Louie beamed. "Why don't you do that? We can always use another good luck charm!"

I felt awful. Good luck charm was my special position. How could Louie be so cruel as to ask Renee to be one, too?

Maybe Louie has a heart after all. Maybe he realized how crummy I was feeling. At any rate, after Marty and Renee had left to go home, he made this marvelous suggestion.

"I have to babysit for my little brother, Jacky, this afternoon," he said. "How about coming along to my house to help me, Linda?"

"Really?" My eyes opened wide. Louie was actually asking me to come to his house! "Sure, I'll come.

That is, if my mother lets me. She's just full of ridiculous restrictions!''

"I'll ask her for you," Danny volunteered. "Your mother trusts me."

With Danny there to plead my case, my mother agreed to let me go to Louie's. But only for one hour. I had to be home so she could "supervise" my lunch. What a pain my mother could be!

Louie's mother was nothing like mine. She looked happy to see Louie bring home some friends. "Sorry I have to run." She smiled warmly as she went out the door. "But you kids just make yourselves at home while I'm gone—there's plenty of food in the refrigerator."

"Yeah, Louie, make me some food. I'm hungry!" a little voice squeaked.

I looked down. There was a miniature Louie.

"This is my little brother, Jacky," Louie said, scooping him up in his arms. "Jacky, say hello to Linda."

"Hi," he said shyly, ramming his thumb into his mouth. "I'm hungry, Louie," he repeated.

"Okay, Jacky." Louie put him down. "Let's see what there is to eat in the kitchen. Come on, Linda."

I followed them into the kitchen and watched while Louie searched through the refrigerator. "Hhmm. Looks like my mother left us hamburgers. How are you at cooking hamburgers, Linda?"

"Great!" I replied. "I've had lots of experience cooking hamburgers." Actually, my experience was limited to the one time I had cooked when my mother was sick. I had burned those hamburgers pretty badly. But I wasn't going to tell Louie that. I figured I could do better this time, anyhow.

"Here's the frying pan." Louie was pulling things out of a cabinet. "Here's the spatula. And here's the oil."

"Oil? What do you need oil for?" I asked.

"Why to fry the hamburgers in, of course," he informed me.

"We don't use oil when we make hamburgers," I insisted. "The hamburger has enough fat of its own."

"Well, I like my hamburgers fried in oil."

"Okay, okay!" I gave in. "It's your stomach. If you want your meat swimming in fat, it's your business. I'll make it any way you want!"

I put the pan on the burner and turned on the gas. Louie poured in the oil and let it heat up. Jacky stood holding Louie's pants leg, still sucking his thumb.

A warm feeling went through me. I could almost imagine that Louie and I were grown up and married and that Jacky was our son. How great it would be to have our own apartment. We could do whatever we wanted. There would be no one to give us orders. We could be together every day. We would cook together just as we were doing now.

The oil began sizzling. The pan was hot. Louie took out the hamburger patties and tossed them into the pan. Hot fat went spattering in all directions.

"Watch out!" Louie yelled, pushing me away. It was too late. Grease stained my shirt from top to bottom. I could feel my lip throbbing where a glob of fat had landed.

"Ow! That hurts!" I said, rubbing the painful spot.

"Don't do that! It will only make it worse," Louie warned. "Here, let me take a look at that." He held my face and tilted it up to the light. I forgot all about the pain.

"A little ice should help that," Danny suggested. Louie went to the freezer and took out a cube.

"Here, hold this on your lip." He placed the ice on my lip and pressed down carefully. I looked up into his eyes.

"Louie! Louie! The hamburgers, Louie! I'm hungry!" Jacky insisted. "You're letting the hamburgers burn!"

Sure enough, smoke was pouring from the pan! I put the ice down and quickly flipped the hamburgers over with the spatula.

"I hope you like your hamburgers well done," I commented. "These look charcoal-broiled!"

"I'll just have to pour on lots of ketchup." Louie laughed.

"You're some cook, Linda!" Danny teased.

"I told him not to use oil," I pouted. "Next time maybe you'll listen to me. Women always know their way around the kitchen better than men do!"

"That's not true, either," Louie insisted. "It's always men who are the greatest chefs!"

I shut off the gas and plopped the burnt burgers down on some paper plates. I guess the boys must have been really hungry, because they ate them, anyhow.

As they were finishing eating, the telephone rang. "It's for you, Linda." Louie handed me the receiver. "Your mother."

I glanced up at the clock. I had been gone almost two hours.

"Hello, Ma," I began feebly.

"Well, Linda? Isn't there a clock in the house you're in?"

"Yes, Ma. But—"

"Didn't you agree to come home in an hour?"

"Yes, Ma—but—I'm sorry."

"Don't, 'I'm sorry' me, Linda! I want you to come home right this instant! Unless you don't want to be allowed out for the rest of the week."

"I'm on my way, Ma!" I hung up the phone and took a deep breath. "I've got to go," I said to Danny and Louie. My face burned with embarrassment at being treated like such a baby in front of the boys.

"Too bad," Louie said with a laugh. "I was just about to ask you to cook another batch of hamburgers!"

"I think I did enough cooking for today," I responded. But now I was laughing, too.

"Well, maybe some other time, then," he grinned.

"Sure!" I said as I threw on my jacket and raced out the door. I ran down the eight flights of stairs. There wasn't time to wait for the elevator if I wanted to escape my mother's wrath.

I arrived home breathless, but happy, ignoring my mother's mumbled disapproval and the blister that was developing on my lip. It had been a great day, but the best of it was that Louie was talking as if we had a future!

Chapter Eight

IN FEBRUARY, THE much-awaited first semester report cards were handed out in homeroom. My heart beat wildly as I stared at the folded piece of paper. Now I would know if all the effort I had put into getting good grades had paid off. I felt I had done well, but you never could tell for sure until the grades were actually in.

Slowly, I unfolded my card. My eyes bulged. There they were, lined up in a row—A's in every one of my classes! I felt like screaming for joy, but managed to contain myself by thinking of Jan.

With a last name of Zieglebaum, Jan was the last to be called up to Ms. Bouton's desk to get her report card. It would ruin everything if Jan wasn't going to be up there with me in the running for the top ten.

"Jan Zieglebaum!" Ms. Bouton finally called. I watched Jan's face carefully as she unfolded her card. "Yippee!" she sang out, waving her card in the air triumphantly. She practically skipped over to my desk. "I did it, Linda—all A's!"

"Me, too," I said, giving her hand a joyful squeeze.

But then Samantha Milken came by to ruin everything. "You couldn't have done any better than I did," she said, waving her report card, with its string of A's, right in my face. "So don't think you're going to beat me out of the top ten without a fight!"

I was too happy about my report card to let Samantha get to me for very long. The way I looked at it, Samantha didn't deserve to get any honors. There had to be a way that Jan and I would pull right ahead of her before the end of the school year.

In the meanwhile, I couldn't wait to tell Jeremy about my report card. Things had returned to normal between us recently, as he hadn't made any further romantic overtures. I decided that I had probably just read too much into what had happened at Christmas.

"This report card clinches it for us," I told him. "Unless we really blow it next term, the only girls who have a shot for the two representatives to the top ten from our class are me, Jan, and that stuck-up Samantha Milken."

"That's great!" Jeremy said enthusiastically. "In fact, it's really an occasion for a celebration!"

"A c-c-celebration?" I asked. Suddenly, this chill feeling of uneasiness clutched at my stomach. I was pretty sure that I didn't want to hear what was coming up next.

"Uh-huh. A celebration. Why don't I take you to the movies next Friday night?" Jeremy said cheerfully. "They're showing this really great movie right here at the school, and we can invite anyone we like."

"Friday night? I—uh—I—" I stopped, unsure of what to say. Jeremy had played it low-key for so long now that this invitation had taken me completely by surprise. If I turned him down cold, it would hurt his feelings. But if I accepted, it might encourage him into thinking I liked him as a boyfriend, which was even worse. If only I could come up with some good excuse! But my mind was a complete blank. I couldn't come up with anything!

"Too bad your parents would never let you downtown so late at night, huh, Linda?" I heard Jan's voice say.

I looked at her in surprise, and then I realized what she was doing—setting me up with the perfect excuse. "Oh, sure—that's right, Jeremy. My parents would never agree to anything like that. I can hardly get them to allow me out in my neighborhood at night. Coming home late from downtown would be out of the question. Especially with the buses and subways the way they are."

"Oh." Jeremy's face fell. "Well, maybe next time we have something going on right after school then?"

"Uh—yeah. Maybe," I said weakly. "Sorry about next Friday." I threw Jan a look of infinite gratitude.

After that, I avoided coming into contact with Jeremy for the rest of the afternoon. But I had a feeling I had only postponed dealing with the problem.

I was very grateful to Jan for coming to my rescue with Jeremy. She really was a good friend to me. I started thinking about her situation a great deal.

In a way, I felt sorry for Jan. It must be terrible to develop so much later than everyone else. The boys in the crowd often made fun of her for being flatchested. Sometimes even we girls teased her, and we were supposed to be her friends! Not that we meant anything by it, but now that I thought about it, the teasing probably hurt Jan's feelings just the same. Maybe that was why she never even put up a fight when her parents made her stay home now more and more.

That bothered me. I was not being the friend I should be to Jan. If we didn't go to a club meeting together after school, I hardly got to see her because she rarely hung around with us anymore. This was because there were usually boys around now, and her parents were so against our hanging around with boys.

Until now I had just accepted this. I hadn't done a thing to help Jan. And after the way Jan had always been such a good friend to me, too. I was really ashamed of myself.

That's when I made the decision to do something really difficult. I would go see Mrs. Zieglebaum, even though she didn't like me very much. I would speak to her in Jan's behalf.

* * *

That very afternoon, I didn't rush home to what had become the hanging out place for our crowd—the candy store on the corner of my block. Instead I went home with Jan.

"This is just like old times, Linda," she said happily as we sat in her kitchen drinking milk and eating cookies. Then we went into her room and read comic books the way we used to do. Jan seemed to be really enjoying having me there doing these things again, but to tell you the truth, I wasn't having much fun at all.

The front door opened. Mrs. Zieglebaum was home. She walked in and paused by Jan's room. "Hello, Jan," she said. "Did you have a nice day at school?" Then she spotted me.

"Oh. Hello, Linda," she said in a voice that was less than friendly. "I haven't seen *you* here for a while." The way she said that made me think she would not like to see me for a while longer.

Still, I was determined to speak up for Jan. I swallowed hard. "I know, Mrs. Zieglebaum. Roz, Fran, and I usually hang around by my house now. We wish Jan would come and be with us more often. It's a lot of fun because a bunch of kids come to the candy store in my building."

Mrs. Zieglebaum scowled. "Fun? A bunch of kids? Hmph! I know exactly what you mean, Linda Berman. You mean boys. Don't you hang around that candy store so you can meet boys?"

I squirmed uncomfortably. "Well, uh—yes, and, uh—no. I mean—we like to be with boys, of course, that's only natural. But we like to be with other girls, too. It's nice to be in a group."

Mrs. Zieglebaum let out a nasty laugh. "Do you really expect me to believe that? I know perfectly well what you have in mind, and I don't want Jan involved in it. She has plenty of time for boys when she's grown up!"

"But—but learning how to deal with boys is part of growing up," I protested weakly. "We're not too young for that."

"Well perhaps you can convince your parents of that, Linda, but you can't convince me. Jan just isn't ready for that type of thing, and she knows it, too. Don't you, Jan?"

I turned and looked at Jan. She was sitting next to me on the bed, pretending she was still reading her comic. She looked up at her mother meekly and said, "I guess," in a little voice I had to strain to hear.

"See!" Mrs. Zieglebaum smiled triumphantly. "So if you want to see Jan after school, Linda, you'll just have to come to our house. Because I'm not going to allow Jan to hang around a street corner with a crowd of boys!" Having said this, she stalked down the hall to her kitchen.

I looked at Jan with dismay, but her face was buried in her comic once again. "Jan," I said. "Do you really feel the way your mother said? Don't you want to hang around with us anymore? Be part of the Gruesome Four?"

Jan blinked and sucked in her breath. "I'm not

sure,'' she said in her squeaky mouse voice, her eyes never leaving the comic book.

I couldn't believe it! Here I had just made a fool out of myself sticking up for her with Mrs. Zieglebaum, and Jan didn't even care if she could hang around with us or not! For a moment, I felt angry at Jan, but then I started feeling sorry for her again. Maybe Jan really wasn't ready for all the changes that were happening to us with the boys. Maybe she just wasn't ready.

Chapter Nine

As JAN STARTED hanging around with us less, Ellen Rossi, this girl Fran knew from junior high, started hanging around with us more. Ellen was on the chubby side, very busty, and not too bright. Fran and Roz liked Ellen, but I wasn't sure I did. She was one of these types that love to flirt, and the one she seemed to do most of her flirting with was Louie!

I decided the best way to handle this was to get Ellen interested in someone else. The boy I had in mind for her was none other than Lenny Lipoff.

Lenny had been acting particularly difficult ever since the time report cards had come out. Rumors had it that he had gotten a lousy report card and was having a hard time with his parents. Whatever the reason, Lenny was always insulting us girls, calling us names like "little punks," and making nasty remarks. But the boys liked Lenny, with his wise guy comedian ways, and always wanted him around. So like it or not, we were stuck with him.

After careful thought, I concluded that the best way to deal with Lenny was to get him to mellow a little by having a girlfriend to focus his energies on. I shared these thoughts with Roz and Fran.

"Fixing up Ellen and Lenny is in all of our best interests," I stated. "She's a born flirt. Just because she's got her eye on Louie now doesn't mean she won't make a play for Danny or Sheldon. We've got to channel her talents somewhere else."

"And you think Lenny is the place to channel them?" Roz asked doubtfully.

"Why not?" I answered. "Ellen mentioned that she thought Lenny was cute, even though he has a big mouth. And knowing Lenny, he'd just love to be seen with Ellen. She's big in the places that he would find important."

"I know," sighed Fran, eyeing her own small chest sadly. "But do you think it will work?"

"We won't know unless we try," I insisted.

We tried to arrange it so that Ellen and Lenny were thrown together as much as possible. The weather was still too cold to be outside for very long. Since the candy store was in our building, we wound up most often at either Danny's or my apartment. Amazingly enough, my mother let us come to my house pretty often. I guess she figured that we might as well be where she could keep an eye on us. She still had these silly rules like no sitting on beds, but it was better to sit on chairs than to freeze on the corner.

After several afternoons of our encouraging the relationship between Ellen and Lenny, they seemed to be really warming up to one another. The big test, however, would be the party we planned at Danny's for Saturday night.

Unfortunately, the party didn't start out quite the way I had wanted it to. When Danny's mother let us in, we found Louie engrossed in reading his SAT review book. He didn't seem to be in much of a partying mood.

This didn't discourage Ellen. She plopped down next to him.

"What are you studying, Louie?" she squeaked. "That looks fascinating! Can I read with you?"

"Sure!" Louie smiled.

I felt my face growing hot with anger. But that was nothing. Within two minutes, Ellen was running her fingers up Louie's back!

I couldn't stand it! I stalked out of Danny's room. There was a mirror hanging in his hall. I stared into it, trying to calm down.

I felt tapping on my shoulder. Lenny was there, looking as mad as I felt.

"For your sake and mine, Linda," he warned, "keep Louie away from Ellen!"

"And how do you expect me to do that?" I demanded angrily. "How about if you keep Ellen away from Louie!"

"Okay, okay. Calm down." He paced back and forth nervously. "We should be working together, not fighting each other. Give me a minute and I'll think of something."

"What if you suggest playing a kissing game? You can arrange it so that you wind up with Ellen."

"Why me? You can suggest one, too," he said.

"It looks better if the suggestion comes from a boy," I insisted.

"Okay, I'll do it," he agreed. "You go back in the room first. I'll come in later. That way it won't look as if we've been plotting together."

"It's a deal!" Feeling better, I opened the door to Danny's room. Roz and Sheldon were standing together by the window, his hand on her shoulder. Danny and Fran were sitting on one end of the bed. His arm was around her.

On the other end of the bed sat Ellen and Louie. His review book was discarded and forgotten. Now she was sitting on his lap!

I felt like running back into the hallway. But Lenny stood back there, out of sight of those in the room. "Get in there!" he whispered through clenched teeth. "Remember our plan!"

I stalked into the room. Ignoring everyone, I went straight to Danny's pile of *Mad* magazines. I pulled one out, sat down cross-legged on the floor, and pretended to read.

Out of the corner of my eye, I could see Ellen running her fingers through Louie's hair. I turned the pages furiously!

Lenny finally came in. He flicked the lights off and on to get everyone's attention. "Let's liven up this party," he announced. "How about a game of Flashlight?"

This was a new game for us, so Lenny explained it. Everyone drew numbers and the girls wound up with the boy with the matching number. One couple held a flashlight and moved it around the darkened room. The object was to kiss your partner and stop before the flashlight could shine on you. If you got caught kissing, the boy would have to take the next turn with the flashlight.

Lenny wrote down four numbers for the boys and four for the girls. I picked number three. I looked hopefully at Louie.

"What's your number, Linda?" he asked.

"Number three. What's yours?" I blinked nervously.

"I've got three, too," he replied.

"No you don't, Louie," Danny protested. "I've got number three." He held it out as proof.

"Oops! I must have misread it!" Louie laughed. "Looks like I've got number two!"

"Ooh! That's my number!" Ellen began jumping up and down.

I gave Lenny a dirty look. He really blew this one! "I'll take the first turn with the flashlight," he volunteered. "I'll try to get them fast," he whispered to me as he shut off the lights.

Danny and I sat down in a corner. Danny started to put his arm around me. Before he could do anything, I started to talk. "Oh, Danny, it's awful! Do you see the way Louie is flirting with Ellen? Do you think he likes her?"

"Don't worry about it, Linda. The way she throws herself at him, there's not much else he can do. I'm sure he likes you better than Ellen."

Danny, having said enough, turned his head to kiss me. I sat up fast. "I hope you're right, Danny. But I've got to see for myself."

I peered through the darkness, trying to see what was happening on the bed. Louie and Ellen were leaning back on some throw pillows. I could make out their arms wrapped around each other. From where I sat, there was no way to tell for sure whether or not they were kissing.

The flashlight switched on. Its beam circled the room and focused on Louie and Ellen. They stayed right where they were, arms entwined.

"Okay! Break it up! I caught you!" Lenny switched on the lights. Louie and Ellen finally sat up.

Lenny walked over and handed Louie the flashlight. "Now you've got to work the flashlight, Louie. And give us some time before you switch it on!"

We drew numbers again. This time I really did wind up with Louie. Just my luck! I knew he'd never kiss me while he was working the flashlight.

As we sat on the bed, he put his arm around me. I was hopeful, but he began playing with the flashlight.

"Are you having fun?" I asked him sarcastically.

He didn't pick up on my meaning. "I guess so. The only problem is that these parties are so immature."

"Immature? What do you mean?"

"Take these silly kissing games, for example. They're fine when you're younger, but at this age, they're silly. If I want to kiss a girl, I will. But I refuse to do so during a kissing game." As if to emphasize his point, he flicked the flashlight on and off.

"Oh," I said. "Well, I agree with you. I don't like to kiss during silly kissing games, either." As I said this I crossed my fingers. I tried to convince myself that I wasn't really telling a lie. After all, I would much rather have Louie kiss me on his own without a kissing game. But at this point, I'd be willing to settle for whatever I could get!

"Let's see. Where should I focus this flashlight?" Louie started swinging it around the room rapidly. I caught brief glimpses of all the other couples. Everyone had wound up with the right partner this time. From what I could see, they were all enjoying themselves.

Fran and Danny were in my old spot on the floor, and Roz and Sheldon were together on the other end of the bed. Across the room, Lenny was sitting on Dan's chair with Ellen on his lap. Louie finally focused the light on them. As it flashed in their faces, I could see Ellen pull back from Lenny's kiss.

"Yuck!" she said loudly enough for me to hear. "Where did you learn to kiss like that?"

Lenny stared at her, then shoved her off his lap. He stood up and turned the lights back on. "I've had enough of these kissing games," he announced. "Have you got anything to eat in this house, Kopler?"

Danny poked his head up from the floor where he

and Fran were still entwined. "There's some ice cream in the freezer. Help yourself."

Lenny headed for the kitchen. Everyone else decided that they were hungry, too. They followed Lenny in.

I pulled Ellen aside. "I heard what you said to Lenny," I told her. "If you want him to like you, why in the world did you tell him that he was a lousy kisser?"

"That's not exactly what I said," she whined. "He was doing something funny with his tongue. It started to tickle. So I just asked him where he learned to kiss that way. It didn't necessarily mean that he's a lousy kisser!"

"Yeah? Well, I also heard you say 'yuck.' That's not exactly a sound of passion, you know."

"But I really didn't mean it that way," she insisted. "I really do like Lenny. He's cute!"

"I'm glad to hear that, Ellen. For a while I thought that you liked Louie." I stared at her accusingly.

"Oh, Louie," she giggled. "He's cute, too. He's real cuddly, but I don't think he likes to play kissing games!"

"Oh?" I replied. "He seemed to be having fun with you from what I saw."

She just giggled again. But from what she said, I didn't think he had kissed her, either.

"Why don't you go into the kitchen and see if you can make up with Lenny?" I suggested. "He looked like he was pretty mad at you."

"I'm sure I can get him to forget about that." She smiled confidently.

I walked behind her to the kitchen. She really wiggled when she walked. Big-busted or not, in my opinion, she was fat.

By the time we got to the kitchen, the entire half-gallon of ice cream had already been divided up.

"Boy, what hogs!" I commented. "No consideration for anyone else!"

"Here, Linda. You can have some of mine," Fran offered.

"And you can share with me, Ellen," Roz volunteered.

"That's okay, Roz," Ellen said. "Lenny has so much. I'm sure he won't mind sharing with me." She walked up to him and put her hand on his shoulder.

Lenny had helped himself to a huge portion of ice cream. For a moment, he looked as if he was going to shove it in Ellen's face. I was hoping that he would.

"Please, Lenny," she purred softly, coming still closer. Lenny swallowed hard. "Well, okay. Just get your own spoon!"

Boy that Ellen had nerve. She grabbed a spoon, plopped down on Lenny's lap, and began shoveling ice cream into her mouth. She ate way more than he did.

I looked at Ellen in disgust. I could never act the pushy way she did with boys. But then again, it seemed to be paying off for her. For once, even loudmouth Lenny had nothing to say!

Chapter Ten

ONE WINDY MARCH day, I was called out of Ms. Bouton's English class to go down to the school office. There, I received notification from Dr. Lilienthal, the principal, that I had passed the test for Bronx Technology.

For a moment, I stood there, blinking, not fully realizing what was happening. Then it hit me.

"I made Bronx Tech! I really made Bronx Tech!" I practically jumped in the air with joy. Now I could go to school with Louie next year, just the way I had planned and dreamed. Jan and I would . . .

"Jan!" It was with a sense of horror that I said her name aloud. "What about Jan Zieglebaum? Why isn't she here? She took the Tech test, too."

"Yes, I know." Dr. Lilienthal sat back behind her desk, a serious expression on her face. "But we're only giving personal notification to those who passed the test. The ones who didn't will hear by mail."

"But—Jan!" I protested weakly, still unable to accept what I knew to be true.

But Dr. Lilienthal was already done with me. "Now run along back to your class," she said, ushering me to the door of her office. "We don't want you to miss out on what Ms. Bouton has to teach you about English, do we? After all, you're going to be our representative of Huntington when you go to Bronx Technology. We want you to do us proud!" Having said this, she closed the door behind me.

I had passed the test for Technology and Jan had not. The reality of the situation hit me as I slowly walked back to class. All my joy at having made Science was now forgotten. Jan and I had done so much talking and planning about how we would go to Science together. She was going to be heartbroken when I told her she wasn't going to be able to go after all.

That was when I decided I wouldn't even tell Jan why Dr. Lilienthal had called me to her office. Instead, I would make up some excuse about having to check something in my records. By the time Jan got her notification in the mail, maybe I could think of something to do.

I opened the door to Ms. Bouton's room, hoping to slip back into my seat unnoticed. No such luck.

"Come over here by my desk and tell the class your good news, Linda," Ms. Bouton said.

I felt an uneasy clutching in my stomach. "G-g-good news? W-what good news?"

"Why your news about making Bronx Technology,

of course! Isn't that why Dr. Lilienthal called you to the office?"

As much as I liked Ms. Bouton, at that moment I could have done without her very well. I squirmed uncomfortably.

"Well—uh—I guess so!" I admitted.

Ms. Bouton looked at me as if I were the world's biggest dummy. Shaking her head in exasperation, she announced, "Dr. Lilienthal told me the good news this morning. Due, undoubtedly, to the superb background that Linda received here at Huntington, she passed the test for the Bronx High School of Technology. I imagine this means you'll be leaving next year, Linda—right?"

"Right," I was about to answer. But then I caught sight of Jan's face. Her normally olive complexion had turned pale, and her big brown eyes stared at me in horror. "I haven't made up my mind yet for sure," was all I could say as I made my way to my seat, brushing off the other girls' expressions of congratulations.

I felt Jan's eyes burning into my back as I sat down in front of her. "What about me?" I heard her squeaky voice say.

For a moment, I was tempted to take the easy way out and lie to her. But that would only make things worse in the long run.

I turned to face Jan, but I couldn't look her directly in the eyes. "They only sent the school word of those who passed the test," I told her. "The ones who didn't will be notified by mail."

"So I didn't make it."

"No."

Jan sat there quietly for what seemed a very long time. "You're going to go off to Tech and leave me alone in Huntington, aren't you, Linda?" she said in a voice so small I could barely hear her.

"I don't know, yet," I answered unhappily. "I still have to talk it over with my parents."

My parents, true to form, made it even more difficult for me. We sat around the kitchen table that night, discussing my school situation.

"You mean you'd abandon Jan, your friend, and go to Bronx Technology by yourself?" My mother got right to the point. This was not what I wanted to hear. I felt bad enough about Jan without my mother's rubbing it in.

"Ma, I'm not abandoning Jan!" I tried to defend myself. "I'm not Jan's only friend in Huntington. In fact, she gets along with the other girls there better than I do."

"That's because she's not boy-crazy like you are," said my father. "She's interested in getting the best education possible, which, I feel, happens to be at Huntington. If you change schools in the middle of a program, you can't help but lose out educationally. You can concentrate on your schoolwork better without the distraction of having boys around."

"That's not true, Daddy," I protested. "I can concentrate just fine with boys around. Maybe even better. Bronx Technology is as good a school as Huntington. You just have to let me go!''

My father drew his eyebrows together in a frown. He looked over at my mother. She just shook her head. I held my breath, waiting for their decision.

"Well, Linda,'' my father said finally. "Your mother and I don't want to force you to stay at Huntington if you think you'll be happier elsewhere. The final decision will be yours. But we want you to keep in mind how we feel when you think about making your decision. We don't want you to jeopardize your education.''

"Or abandon your friends,'' my mother added.

I nodded miserably. When it came to making me feel guilty, my parents knew exactly what to say. Jan and I had been friends for years. She had always counted on me to stick up for her and give her courage. If I went to Tech, I really would be abandoning Jan, and she was the most loyal friend anyone could ask for.

But not going to Tech meant having to stay at Huntington, where I wasn't really that happy. It meant not going to school with boys. But worst of all, it meant not going to school with Louie. What was I going to do?

I watched Louie's face carefully when I told him I passed the test for Bronx Technology. It was important to me that he would want me to go. But as usual, his expression was impossible to read.

"I still haven't decided whether or not to go,'' I said

slowly, still watching his face. "My parents want me to stay at Huntington."

For a moment he said nothing. Then he shrugged. "Well, I guess you have to suit yourself, Linda. But if you ask me, you'd be crazy to turn down going to Tech. After all, I go there!"

He grinned when he said that, and it was as if the sun came out from behind a cloud. His eyes twinkled the way I loved. I felt my heartbeat speed up.

That was when I knew what my decision had to be. As bad as I felt about Jan, there was nothing I could do about the fact that she didn't make Tech. Jan had been dependent on me for a long time. If she was going to grow up, she would have to learn to stand up for herself.

Looking at it that way, by going to Tech, I was actually doing Jan a favor.

I couldn't seem to convince Jan of that, however. We were standing in the hallway after school when I told her my decision. Her large brown mouse-eyes filled with tears.

"I'll never see you if we don't go to school together," she said sadly.

"Sure you will, Jan."

"Like when?"

"Like—uh—well." I felt awful. I didn't know what to say. Jan was right. Since she hardly ever hung around with our crowd anymore, about the only time I did see her was in school. "I'm sure we'll find some time to spend together. On the weekends, maybe—times when the boys aren't around, so your mother won't mind.''

"But you're always hanging around with boys now, Linda. You, Fran, and Roz. Sometimes I think that's all you ever think of—boys.''

I stared at her in surprise. "What do you mean, Jan?''

She swallowed. "Just what I said. Once we all used to do things together as a group, and it was lots of fun. Sure we liked boys, and that was fine, because we did other things that were fun, too—playing ball, reading comics, listening to music, or just talking together. But it's not like that anymore. Unless there are boys around, none of the rest of you remember how to have fun!'' Jan's eyes filled with accusation.

I shrank under her piercing gaze. Could Jan be right? Were we all so boy-crazy that we no longer knew any other way to have fun? I didn't think so, but I could see where it might seem that way to Jan. She was the one who was always being left out.

"I didn't know you felt that way, Jan," I said.

"Well, I do. So you can have Bronx Technology, Linda, and all the boys, too! I'll be just fine here at Huntington. And now, I've got to get going to my art club meeting. You know, the one you didn't join with me because you were more interested in spending the time hanging around with the boys!''

Throwing her bookbag over her frail little shoulder, Jan took off down the hall. She left me speechless. I guess, in her own way, Jan was more grown up than any of us gave her credit for being.

Chapter Eleven

LOUIE SEEMED TO look at me with more interest once he knew I was going to Tech. We spent a lot of time together up at Danny's. We did silly things like read *Mad* magazines, or we studied or watched TV together.

I kept watching Louie for signs that he liked me. Sometimes he acted as if he did and sometimes he didn't. It was all very confusing.

I figured that the perfect opportunity to find out how he really felt about me was going to be at a party we were invited to at Marty's house. Renee Berkley was going to be there. Even though she was still going out with Marty, Renee was ready to fall all over Louie any chance she got.

Not only was Renee coming, but Ellen Rossi was invited, too. Of course, supposedly she was coming with Lenny, but Ellen wasn't one to let that stand in the way of her shameless flirtations with Louie.

Ellen and Renee—double opportunity for trouble. If Louie chose to be with me at the party despite their presence, I could feel reasonably sure that he liked me best.

But things didn't work out the way I planned.

The first thing that went wrong was that Roz wasn't able to come. Her father was punishing her because she left her just-washed pantyhose dripping in the bathroom. It seems he slipped on the puddle that had formed. He didn't hurt himself, but was mad because she had dared to laugh at the way he looked lying on the floor!

The next thing that went wrong was that Ellen and Lenny had a big fight. Ever since that time at Danny's, Lenny refused to kiss Ellen. She was always playing little games to tease him and to try to get him to kiss her. She would do things like creep her fingers up his arm and around his back. She always wound up with her lips right near his. Still, he refused to kiss her.

I guess she teased him one time too many. The way I heard the story, he wound up grabbing her in a place she didn't want to be grabbed. She promptly slapped his face. At any rate, Lenny was not coming to the party.

When we got to the party, we found that Marty's parents were out for the night. That was the third thing that went wrong.

"I can't stay here," I said, starting to put my coat back on. "I promised my parents that I wouldn't go to unchaperoned parties."

"What! Are you some kind of baby or something?"

Marty looked angry. "I went to all this trouble to arrange everything, and now you say that you can't stay! It's ridiculous! You're going to ruin the whole party! Don't you trust us?"

"It's not that I don't trust you," I tried feebly to explain. "It's just that I promised my parents. They'd kill me if they found out!"

"How would they find out, anyway?" Louie asked. "No one here would tell them."

I started weakening.

"Please, Linda," begged Fran. "If you leave, I'll have to leave, too."

I looked at everyone. They were all awaiting my decision. Since the other two couples weren't coming, it was only Marty and Renee, Danny and Fran, and Louie and I at the party. It certainly would ruin the party if Fran and I left. It would really be a rotten thing to do to Marty.

"Oh, all right. I'll stay." I took off my coat again. "I just hope my parents don't find out about this!"

We had just started dancing when the doorbell rang. Marty went to the door. We heard voices arguing and rushed to see who was there. It was Lenny, Nicky, Norman, and Sheldon, trying to crash our party. They were acting loud and crazy. Marty slammed the door.

"I'm not letting those guys in," he told us. "They're acting like they're looking for trouble!"

"Trouble?" Renee hung on to him. "I'm frightened, Marty! What do you think they might do?"

"They're not going to do anything," Marty answered. "I'm just not going to let them in. Come on, let's start dancing again." He led the way back to the living room.

I was dancing with Louie and just starting to relax, when the doorbell rang again. Everyone froze. We all looked at one another.

"I'll handle this," Marty said, going to the door. He put the chain on this time so it could only open a crack. We heard him talking but didn't know what he was saying.

He closed the door behind him.

"What do they want now?" I asked.

"They claim that they'll leave us alone if we just let Sheldon in," he answered. "He's got Ellen with him. He says that since they were both originally invited, we ought to at least let them in."

"Ellen? If Ellen's out there, you've got to let them in!" Fran insisted. "We can't leave her out there with all those boys when they're acting wild like that."

"Why not?" I scowled. "She's probably enjoying every minute of it!" Renee hadn't been a problem so far. The last one I wanted around to make trouble was Ellen!

Everyone else, however, seemed to agree with Fran, so Marty took the chain off the door. Ellen came in, followed by Sheldon.

The next thing we heard were shouts. The rest of the boys tried to force their way in! Nicky led the way. I could see his gawky head coming through the doorway!

"Get out of here, Glick!" Marty yelled, pushing

Nicky in the face. Nicky backed off, and Marty slammed the door shut, locking it behind him.

We could hear the boys yelling out in the hall. "I'll get even with you, Marty! No one calls me Glick and gets away with it. You've got to come out of there sometime! I'll smash you to pieces! I'll make you wish you were never born!" Nicky had obviously flipped out.

Ellen giggled nervously at all this. "What does 'Glick' mean, anyhow?" she asked. "Why does it make him so mad?"

"No one knows," Danny told her. "But you shouldn't have called him that, Marty. He's been known to go crazy over being called Glick before. I wonder what those guys will pull now. They're capable of waiting down there all night!"

I shivered. "This is what happens when you go to unchaperoned parties," I said.

"Oh, stop it, Linda," Fran said with annoyance. "We're here already, so let's try to enjoy it!" She took Dan's hand and led him over to the sofa.

I went and sat on the other sofa. I hoped Louie would sit next to me. He did, but Ellen sat on his other side with Sheldon next to her.

Marty shut the lights off. I couldn't see a thing for a moment. I could her rustling sounds coming from where Ellen and Sheldon were sitting. I wondered if Sheldon was fooling around with Ellen. Did he care so little for Roz that as soon as she wasn't around, he'd go right for Ellen?

95

"Ooh, Louie! That tickles!" I heard Ellen giggle. "Hold my hand, don't play with it!" My heart dropped. It wasn't Sheldon who was fooling around with Ellen. It was Louie!

So this was it. I had wanted proof of how Louie felt, and now I had it. He was obviously choosing Ellen over me. Tears burned my eyes. I tried sniffling them back, but they kept on coming uncontrollably.

I don't know if Louie heard me crying or just sensed that I was upset. But at that moment his hand touched my shoulder. Then his arm went around me, and he pulled me back into his arms.

I couldn't believe it! I quickly wiped my eyes and snuggled up to him. It was the most wonderful feeling to be so close to Louie. He must like me; he must!

Louie's face was right up against mine. I was afraid to breathe. Was he finally going to kiss me?

But before anything could happen, the lights in the living room were suddenly flipped on. I practically jumped out of Louie's arms. What could be the matter now?

"I just checked the hall," Marty announced. It was he who had turned the lights on. "It looks as if those crazy jerks left for a while. I hate to do this, but I think we should take advantage of that fact and clear out of here while the going is good."

Everyone seemed to agree that this was the best thing to do. We grabbed our jackets and filed out into the hallway to make our escape. Our worst fear was that the boys might be waiting for us when we got downstairs. With loudmouth Lenny to work up an already crazed Nicky, anything could happen!

We all herded into the small elevator. I felt my stomach turning as the elevator dropped. I kept praying that there would be no one in the downstairs hall to make trouble when we got there!

The elevator door slid open. My prayers were not answered. Nicky's head towered above us. He looked furious!

"Where's the one who called me Glick?" he asked, smacking his fist into the palm of his hand.

"Come on, Nicky." Sheldon tried to calm him down. "Marty didn't mean it."

Nicky shoved Sheldon aside as if he were a piece of paper. He grabbed Marty by the collar and picked him up off the floor!

"Don't you ever call me Glick again!" he roared. Then he pulled back his arm and punched Marty in the face!

Renee screamed. The doors to the other apartments opened as people tried to see where all the noise was coming from.

"Run, girls, run!" Ellen yelled.

"Maybe we should help Marty," I said, shivering.

"Don't be a fool, Linda," Fran shouted. "There's nothing we could do, anyhow!"

She was right. We girls ran out to the street. We stood there nervously until the boys finally joined us. Blood was dripping from the corner of Marty's mouth.

"Marty, are you all right?" Renee asked tearfully.

"Yeah, I'm okay." He dabbed at the blood with a tissue. "Those guys are really crazy!"

"Where's Sheldon?" I asked. He hadn't come out with the boys.

"He stayed with them to calm them down," Danny said, putting his arms around Fran and me. "Come on, let's get out of here. We'll walk you girls home."

"Well, I learned something tonight," I announced when we reached our building.

"What's that?" Danny asked.

"Sometimes my parents aren't so old-fashioned after all. I don't think I want to go to any more unchaperoned parties for a long time!"

"Are you sure about that?" Louie winked at me, his eyes laughing.

I looked into his eyes and remembered how his arms felt around me. "Well, we'll just have to be more careful next time," I said. Boy, when it came to Louie, I really had no will power at all!

Chapter Twelve

AFTER THE LONG cold winter, we welcomed the first signs of spring. As the air warmed, the city had a special smell that filled me with joy. Now we spent as much time as possible outside, usually by my corner or the park wall, which overlooked the baseball field.

The park was beautiful in the springtime. It was one of the only places in our part of the city where the true miracle of spring could be observed. The poor trampled grass that was so brown and lifeless during the winter suddenly came alive again. Little buds burst from barren branches on bushes and trees, and dandelions came up overnight. Birds returned and resumed their singing. Best of all, the boys started playing baseball again.

That meant there was always something happening in the park. On weekend mornings when there was no bowling, I would fly through my chores and race to the park. I didn't want to miss any action.

On this Sunday, I arrived before the game started. A crowd of boys huddled excitedly behind the batter's cage. Sheldon, Lenny, Norman, and Nicky were there. I climbed over the park wall and dropped to the field below, anxious to see what was happening.

Lenny stood talking in the center of the crowd. "Tell us what happened next," I heard Sheldon urge him.

Lenny threw back his head. His eyes flashed with life. Obviously, he was enjoying telling his story. I couldn't understand why. It was this whole long thing about how his parents had gotten so mad at him that they both began hitting him at once. His response was to run away from home. He had taken a bus all the way to Philadelphia and back again. He had stayed out the whole night, too. He had climbed up the fire escape that led to Nicky's room, climbed in the window, and he had spent the night sleeping under Nicky's bed. His parents had been so worried about him that when he called home in the morning, they promised not only never to hit him again but to give him extra spending money.

"So I'm on my way home right now," Lenny concluded. "See you guys later." He made a dramatic exit, climbing over the park wall and disappearing down the street.

Everyone stared after him. For a moment we were all speechless.

"Boy," I said finally. "I can't believe that Lenny. He acts as if he's proud of doing a stupid thing like that!"

"Don't be so hard on Lenny," Sheldon said to me. "He lives in a house with parents that don't get along. His father's not home half the time, and when he is, there's always screaming and fighting. So Lenny acts like a big shot and pretends he doesn't care. But underneath it all, he's really hurting."

"Oh," I said, suddenly ashamed of myself for not being more understanding. "I guess you're right, Sheldon. I mean, I always thought it was tough to have parents that are old-fashioned. I don't know what I'd do if I had to live with parents like Lenny's!"

I made up my mind to be nicer to Lenny—if only he'd let me!

But by the very next weekend, Lenny was causing trouble again. We all went up to Ellen Rossi's house on Saturday afternoon. Ellen was teasing the boys in her usual flirty way. Actually, she was really asking for what happened next.

Lenny gathered the boys together to talk. I couldn't hear what he was saying, but I could see he was stirring up trouble from the expression on his face.

When the boys came back, they all attacked Ellen. Nicky and Lenny held her arms, and Sheldon and Danny held her legs. "Now get her, Louie!" Lenny yelled. "Start tickling her!"

Ellen began screaming and squirming. She hated to be tickled. Louie was having a hard time getting to her.

Fran, Roz, and I ran to Ellen's rescue. Roz and

Fran tried to pull Sheldon and Danny off her legs, while I hammered my fists on Louie's back.

"Get away from Ellen!" I yelled.

"Hey, that hurts!" Louie backed away from Ellen, rubbing his spine where I had hit him. "You didn't have to hit so darn hard, Linda!" He looked really angry when he said that.

Things quieted down after that. But Louie seemed annoyed at me for the rest of the afternoon. This got me worried. Because earlier, Sheldon had invited us to come to his house that night for what was supposed to be a party for couples: himself and Roz, Danny and Fran, and Louie and me. I was really looking forward to this party. But if Louie was still angry, it could ruin the entire evening.

Never in my wildest dreams could I have imagined that the party would have turned out the way it did. I knew something was wrong right from the beginning when Louie, who was always on time, still hadn't shown up a half hour after the party started.

At first, everyone hung around the kitchen, waiting for Louie to arrive. Finally, Danny and Fran, who had gotten pretty serious about each other recently, went and sat on one of the two sofas in the living room.

They started kissing. Roz and Sheldon were obviously anxious to follow suit. I stood there by the snack table, nervously eating potato chips and pretzels one after another. Where was Louie?

Just when I thought I couldn't stand it any longer,

the doorbell rang. Sheldon went to answer it and came back with Louie. My heart hammered fearfully.

"Join the party, Louie," said Sheldon. He plopped down on a sofa and gave Roz a meaningful look. Roz glanced at me to make sure I was okay. I looked at Louie.

But Louie was acting as if I wasn't even there. He walked right by me and went straight to the snack table. "Oh, good, potato chips!" he commented. "I'm starved!" He picked up the entire bowl and sat down on a chair. Then he turned on the radio and started singing along with it.

Roz watched all this. Then she walked over to Louie and said, "Why don't you act normal, Louie?"

"I'll act any way I want to," he replied rudely. The way he wanted to was to sit on the chair looking at the ceiling. He kept on singing with the radio.

"I give up!" Roz sighed. She went over and sat on the sofa next to Sheldon. After a while, they started kissing, too.

So the party I had longed for turned into a nightmare. Louie sat there on the chair while I sat on the floor in a corner of the room.

Tears burned my eyes. At first I struggled to hold them back, but then they started rolling down my cheeks faster than I could control. Once I began crying, I found I couldn't stop. It was awful!

Louie didn't have to say anything to me. I knew that he was showing me that whatever we once had going between us was now over. But I didn't understand why he had to pick this horrible way of doing it. Didn't he know how embarrassed I would be to be rejected like this in front of my friends? Didn't he care? How could he be so cruel?

Louie kept it up the entire evening. I felt like a real fool sitting there on the floor, but I didn't have the guts to get up and leave by myself.

I sat there listening to the sound of Louie's voice singing softly with the radio. Thoughts of how wonderful it had once been to have him hold me in his arms kept floating through my head. When I thought of how great I had hoped tonight would be, it was more than I could take. I sobbed so hard I thought my body would burst.

I used up a whole box of Sheldon's tissues that night. Louie had to have known how terrible I was feeling. But he never even looked my way.

When the party finally broke up, Sheldon and Roz walked me home. "I don't know why Louie did this." Sheldon tried to cheer me up. "I always thought he liked you best of all the girls."

I tried to smile. "Thanks, Sheldon. It really doesn't matter anymore. If it's over, it's over. I'll be all right." I walked sadly to my building.

Once they had left me alone, I didn't feel so brave. I just couldn't bring myself to go up to my apartment. What if my parents were still up? I didn't want them to see me with my nose all swollen and my eyes all red from crying.

I sat down on the stoop in front of my building. I needed to be alone. It was really over. It hurt so bad! My stomach ached and my chest felt like exploding. I started crying all over again. It seemed to release some of the terrible pressure I felt inside.

Lenny and Nicky walked by. I tried to stifle my crying, but I guess they heard me.

"What's the matter with you, Linda?" Lenny asked, a shocked expression on his face.

"It's L-L-Louie!" I sobbed, shaking my head. I could hardly speak. "W-What he did to me tonight!"

"What did he do to you? I'll break his head if he touched you!" Nicky threatened, putting up his fists.

"No, it wasn't anything like that!" Despite everything, I had to laugh at how funny Nicky looked. I swallowed hard and told them the story of the evening.

"That dirty rat!" Lenny said, putting his arm around me. "Let's go into your building and talk."

We went in and sat on the staircase. Lenny was really nice to me. He told me about how bad he had felt when Ellen broke up with him. "For a while I didn't want to be anywhere that she was," he said. "I got over it, and you will, too."

"Do you really think so?" I sniffled. Somehow, talking to Lenny was making me feel a lot better. I hadn't known he was capable of being so caring, so understanding.

Nicky had been waiting outside while we were talking. Now he came running into the hall. "Louie's here!" he announced. "I just saw him coming around the corner."

"Oh, no," I moaned. "I don't think I can stand facing him now!"

"I'll take care of Louie," Lenny assured me. He

got up as Louie entered the hall. "Hey Louie," he said, pulling some coins out of his pocket. "Here's some money. Go treat yourself to a soda. You deserve it for being such a great guy!"

Louie took the money and grinned this sheepish grin. "Boy you're generous tonight, Lipoff. Feeling all right?"

"We'll all feel a lot better when you get lost!"

Louie laughed. He left the building and walked toward the candy store.

"That Louie is as cold and heartless as they come," Lenny commented. "You don't know it yet, Linda, but you're really going to be better off without him!"

Chapter Thirteen

For an entire week, no one would talk to Louie. It was hard to keep that up when he kept coming around. Little by little, people began talking to him again.

I didn't want to see him at all. If we had to be in the same room, I made sure to be as far from him as possible. I acted hurt and got a lot of sympathy for a while. This soon became tedious. People got tired of giving me sympathy. I started feeling more comfortable with Louie around. Time began to heal my wounds.

Things returned to normal. I found I was even able to joke around with Louie as if nothing had happened. Almost. There was still the pain of rejection, but I covered it up pretty well.

The worst part was having no boyfriend when my friends all did. Roz and Sheldon, and Dan and Fran were still going strong. Ellen and Lenny got back together. Louie was spending a lot of time with busty

Renee Berkley, who had stopped dating Marty. Only I had no one. It was awful!

During Easter vacation, our crowd planned a trip to an amusement park. The boys were even going to pay for the girls. I decided not to go.

"Come on, Linda. You don't need a boyfriend to have fun in an amusement park," Danny urged. We were sitting in his house, discussing the trip.

"Maybe not," I answered. "But when everyone else is paired off, I'd feel pretty stupid by myself."

"Are you sure it's not the fact that Louie is taking Renee Berkley that's keeping you from coming?" Fran asked.

"Of course not," I lied. "He's just out for what he can get from her anyhow. She's welcome to him!"

"Then come with us," insisted Fran. "I'd feel terrible if you stayed home by yourself."

"I'd be by myself even if I went with you," I pointed out.

"Maybe not," commented Lenny. He had been listening to our conversation with amusement. Now he smiled as if he knew something we didn't know.

"What do you mean, Lenny?" I wanted to know.

"Don't say that I told you anything," he laughed.

"I won't. I won't!"

"I've heard rumors that Nicky might be interested in taking you."

"Nicky?" I stared in amazement. Somehow, I couldn't see Nicky with any girl, least of all me. He was so big and gawky. "Nicky and me?"

"Sure. Why not?" Lenny asked.

"Well, for one thing, he's over a foot taller than I am. We'd look ridiculous together. I can just picture us!" I laughed.

"So what?" Lenny answered. "Nicky doesn't have anyone to go with and neither do you. It wouldn't be so terrible if you went to the amusement park with him. You'd make Nicky feel good, and you might even have a good time yourself."

Put that way, the idea seemed to make sense. So I wound up joining the crowd and going to the amusement park with Nicky.

It started out to be a lot of fun. Nicky bought me a soda and some cotton candy. I got all sticky trying to eat it.

We went on the roller coaster. I liked it so much that I went on three times. The highest hill was the best. The suspense built up as the car slowly climbed to the top. Then—whoosh! Your stomach dropped as the car flew to the bottom.

After the roller coaster, I felt as if I could tackle any ride in the park. "Let's go on that ferris wheel next," I begged.

"I don't know, Linda," Nicky said. "That's not an ordinary ferris wheel. Those cars flip upside down."

"So what." I laughed. "You're not chicken, are you?"

Nicky pulled himself up to his full six feet, two inches. "Of course not. I was just concerned for you."

"So let's go!" I pulled him toward the ticket booth.

The ferris wheel started up. From the top, I had a tremendous view of the amusement park. We were riding locked in a little cage. I started rocking it for excitement.

"Cut that out!" Nicky shouted. "You're going to flip the whole thing over!"

"Isn't that what's supposed to happen?" I laughed, rocking even harder. Sure enough, I got the cage to flip upside down. Once it started flipping, it became impossible to control the cage. It flipped over and over again.

The first time it happened, it was fun. I liked the feeling of being upside down. The second time, I started feeling the cotton candy in my stomach. By the third time we flipped over, I was sure that I was going to throw up!

"Nicky! Stop the car! I'm going to be sick!" I shrieked.

"I can't!" he yelled. "You'll just have to wait until the ride is over."

"Oh no," I groaned. "I don't think I'm going to make it!"

Fortunately, I lasted until the ride stopped. If I had thrown up while we were still spinning, it would have been a terrible mess!

I staggered over to a bench and let my head hang between my knees. I was so nauseous! Then I began heaving. Up came the cotton candy and the soda. Up came the lunch I had eaten hours before!

My stomach felt better, but I was miserable. People were staring at me as they walked by. What a sight I must have been!

Nicky was really terrific. He brought me some napkins to clean myself up with and some water to drink.

We moved to another bench. "Why don't you just rest a little," he suggested.

I nodded my head. I was too exhausted for conversation. I was also too exhausted to protest when he put his arm around me. How could I when he had been so nice to me?

Nicky kept his arm around me on the long ride home. At this point, it seemed really awkward to say anything. Besides, Louie had his arm around Renee Berkley, and I wanted to get even!

Nicky walked me home from the bus. "Are you sure you're okay, Linda?" he asked at my door.

"Yeah." I smiled sheepishly. "It was pretty dumb of me to act like that in the amusement park. Thanks for putting up with me."

"Putting up with you? I had a good time!" Nicky looked into my eyes. "I'll see you tomorrow, won't I?"

"Sure," I answered, fumbling with my key.

"Good! And maybe we can go up to Danny's on Saturday. I hear some couples are going to be there." Nicky looked at me just like a lonesome puppy.

"Oh! Well, uh, I guess so. I mean, we'll see. See you!" I slammed the door behind me and leaned up against it. I took a deep breath.

Now what was I going to do? Nicky liked me, that was obvious. He was nice, but there was no way I wanted him for a boyfriend. Yet, I didn't want to do anything to hurt his feelings. I had just gotten myself into another difficult situation.

After that, everyone thought of Nicky and me as a couple. This created some problems for me. While I basically liked Nicky and didn't mind going places with him in a group, when it came to the two of us alone, it was a disaster.

The worst was when we wound up alone with the other couples in someone's house. Nicky would put his arm around me and look at me with that puppy dog look that meant he wanted to kiss me. Sometimes he would get brave and try. I would turn my head and duck down into his neck. I could tolerate having Nicky's arm around me; it was warm and cuddly. But I didn't like him enough to want to kiss him.

I didn't know what to do. I didn't want to hurt Nicky's feelings, but I didn't want to be his girlfriend. The thought hit me that this could have been the way Louie had felt about me. How awful! Maybe the way he had acted that night was the only way he knew to end a relationship that was going nowhere.

What Louie had done hurt, but I got over it. Maybe what I was doing to Nicky was even crueler. I decided to end it.

That was easier said than done. I started by acting cool to him and dropping little hints. He refused to take them. I became irritable and snappy. He just laughed good-naturedly. Sometimes I was downright nasty. Nothing semed to discourage him.

"I feel like a real crumb for the way I'm acting," I

confided to Fran one day. "But I don't know what to do!"

We were sitting on the park wall on a gorgeous May day. The yellow haze of New York pollution had lifted, and the sky was bright blue. The sun was warm enough so we didn't even need a sweater. I should have been feeling wonderful.

"I don't want the relationship to go on any longer," I continued. "But I don't want to hurt Nicky the way Louie hurt me."

Fran looked thoughtful. "Don't you think you're hurting him even worse this way? It's like having a Band-Aid pulled off. You can do it in one quick motion or a little at a time. It hurts either way, but I'd rather have it over with fast!"

I thought about that. "You're right, Fran. But I have been giving him hints, you know. He just doesn't pick up on them. The situation drags on and on."

Fran jumped down from the wall angrily. "Do you know something, Linda? I don't think you really want to end the relationship either. I think you're afraid of being alone without a boyfriend."

What she said hit me over the head like a hammer. The awful feeling of being alone while all my friends had boyfriends came back to me. Fran was right. I hadn't made a real effort to end it with Nicky. Being with him was still better than being by myself.

"You're right, Fran," I admitted. "I've only been fooling myself. I've been totally unfair to Nicky. You are my witness. I'm going to end this thing before the weekend is over!"

* * *

On Saturday afternoon, Nicky and Lenny rang my bell. Instead of asking them in, I stood in the doorway with my arm blocking the way.

"Hi," I said sullenly.

"Hi, Linda!" Nicky smiled warmly. He didn't seem to notice that I was blocking the doorway.

"What do you want?" I asked, without smiling.

"We're going to pick up some snacks for the party at Danny's," Nicky said happily. "We thought you'd want to come to the store with us."

"No, I'm not going," I said flatly.

Nicky's face fell. Lenny stared at me. I felt awful. I didn't know if I could go through with this.

"Oh, you can't come out now." Nicky tried smiling again. "Well, then I guess I'll call for you tonight on the way to Danny's."

My stomach growled. I didn't have enough guts to do it. I remembered my oath to Fran. How much longer could I drag out pulling off the Band-Aid?

"No, Nicky. You don't understand. I'm not going with you tonight either." I swallowed hard. "It's over."

Nicky stared at me. His mouth was open and his face was a blank. Lenny's face was easier to read. He got red and his veins stood out the way they did when he got angry. My eyes dropped to the floor.

"Come on, Nicky!" Lenny put his hand on Nicky's shoulder. "Let's get out of this stinking place!"

I closed the door behind me. I felt an immediate sense of relief. It was done!

114

I ran and looked out the window. Lenny and Nicky were walking up the block. Lenny still had his arm on Nicky's shoulder. Lenny was talking and talking. It seemed that he was always there to pick up the pieces whenever I was involved in a breakup. Only this time, he wasn't feeling sorry for me. This time, he thought I was a rat.

I felt awful! I flopped down on my bed and started to cry. In a way, this was as painful as breaking up with Louie. Now, just as then, I was faced with being alone without a boyfriend. But at least then, I wasn't angry at myself.

Chapter Fourteen

JUST WHEN I thought that my problems with boys who liked me as girlfriends while I liked them only as friends were over, Jeremy hit me with a new one. He asked me to go with him to the Manhattan School's end-of-the-year prom.

"Prom?" I repeated in disbelief. "You—you're asking me to your prom?"

"Uh-huh." Jeremy's face blushed slightly. "There's no one I'd rather take than you, Linda. And since I know your parents wouldn't let you come downtown by yourself at night, I've fixed it so you can be picked up and brought back home by taxi. That should take care of that problem. So what do you say, Linda? Will you come?"

"I—uh—I—" I fumbled. That familiar uncomfortable feeling clutched at my stomach once again. I had just about gotten to the point where I could face Nicky after what had happened. The last thing I needed was

116

for Jeremy to start making romantic overtures to me again. This time, Jan wasn't around to get me out of it, either. "I—I'll have to ask my parents," I managed to say. At least that way, I was buying some time until I could think of something.

You can bet that if it was something I was really dying to go to, my parents would have refused to let me go to the prom. But they decided that it would be good for me to attend a prom with "less fortunate children"—a sort of educational experience. So I was back to coming up with my own solution.

My first reaction was to quit the service club so I wouldn't have to face Jeremy at all. Even though that would disqualify me from the top ten at Huntington, now that I was going to Bronx Technology next year, it really shouldn't matter.

But it did matter. For one thing, my parents were still disappointed that I was changing schools. If I left Huntington with an honor like being in the top ten, it would make them feel better about me. It would also make me feel better about myself.

And there was still Samantha Milken. She was doing as well in school as I was, and she had kept up with all her clubs. The last thing I wanted to do was to hand my place in the top ten over to Samantha.

No, running away from the service club wasn't the answer. But what was? I didn't want to go to the prom with Jeremy. But I didn't want to turn him down and hurt his feelings either.

I decided to consult with Danny to get a boy's viewpoint on the matter.

Danny wasted no time telling me what he thought. Like a true big brother, he sat me down and gave it to me straight.

"Don't think you're doing Jeremy a favor by going to the prom with him if you don't like him as a boyfriend, Linda. Why get the guy's hopes up only to have him come up with nothing? Neither of you are going to wind up having a good time if you go without really wanting to. And, for all you know, there's a girl who really wants to go with Jeremy to the prom—someone who really does like him. If you bow out gracefully, you're giving him the chance to find out."

"Kind of like what happened with you and Fran?" I said.

"Exactly." He grinned and tousled my hair. "I'm eternally grateful to you for that one. Although it wouldn't have been so terrible if it had worked out with you and me either. Maybe it still could!" He gazed into my eyes with longing, just the way he used to.

"Danny!" I shrieked in horror. "Don't complicate my life even further!"

But then I saw he was laughing at me. I laughed, too. It was great to be able to laugh over something that once was so painful.

I knew I couldn't wait much longer to give Jeremy my answer. Not if I wanted to give him time to ask someone else to the prom. So the very next day, I stopped off at the Manhattan School. I found Jeremy where I expected to—working on a painting in the art room.

For a moment I stood there, watching him work. With his straight nose and dark, curly hair, Jeremy really did have a handsome profile. He was good-natured, kind, and talented, too. In fact, Jeremy would have been absolutely perfect—if only he could see.

The thought made me feel ashamed. Was it just the fact that Jeremy was blind that kept me from liking him as a boyfriend?

I sighed. I really didn't know how I would feel if things were different and Jeremy could see. I only knew that whatever chemistry was necessary to make my heart go flying the way it had with Louie just wasn't there with Jeremy.

I guess Jeremy must have heard me, because he turned to me and smiled. "Linda?" he asked hopefully.

"Uh-huh," I answered. I forced myself to walk into the room. Somehow I managed to get the words out. Something about how I didn't think I was the right one to go with him to the prom. That I was sure he would find someone else to go who would really appreciate it.

I don't think it would have mattered what words I had chosen. The hurt in Jeremy's face would have been there no matter what.

"Sure, I understand," he said to me. But I could tell he didn't really.

There was nothing further I could say. With a, "See you, Jeremy," I turned and fled from the building. I was just glad there were only a few more weeks left of school in which I had to face him.

That weekend, the temperature climbed. Our crowd decided it was time to attempt a pilgrimage to the ocean. We decided to get together and hit Rockaway Beach.

It was a two-hour subway ride from our neighborhood out to Rockaway. But once you got there, it was worth it. The water was clean, there were waves to jump, and there was an amusement area with games to play.

Wouldn't you know it, I got stuck sitting next to Lenny Lipoff on the train. If it wasn't for the fact the ride was so long, I would have gotten up and stood the whole trip. Because Lenny had been especially difficult recently. He and Ellen had broken up again, and he was so nasty to her that she had stopped hanging around with our crowd altogether. He was nasty to me, too, because he was still angry at the way I had treated Nicky.

But I wasn't going to let Lenny and his big mouth keep me from enjoying this day at the beach. Since I was sitting next to him, I decided to take the opportunity to talk to him and try to straighten things out.

The subway makes a lot of noise. If you want to carry on a conversation, you have to practically shout. Lenny didn't even bother to make the effort. He sat, beach gear by his feet, reading a sports magazine. He certainly wasn't making it easy for me to talk to him.

"Lenny!" I finally got up the courage to say.

There was no answer. He probably didn't hear me.

"Lenny!" I yelled it this time. He looked at me and blinked.

"Lenny, I'd like to talk to you. Could you please listen a minute?"

He put down his magazine and looked at me as if I were a real pain. "What do you want?" he asked irritably.

I took a deep breath. "You know, Lenny," I began. "Ever since I ended it with Nicky, you've been acting as if I've got the plague or something. I want you to know that it really bothered me to have to break up with him that way. I just didn't know how to do it any other way."

He stared at me with a look of scorn and disbelief. "Yeah, sure," he said. He picked up his magazine again.

I caught his arm. It had been hard enough for me to start this conversation. He was just going to have to let me finish it!

"Be reasonable, Lenny! I didn't like Nicky as a boyfriend. It wouldn't have helped to let it drag on. He would have been hurt even worse that way. Remember how hurt I was over Louie?"

"Well, that should have made you go easier with Nicky. You hurt him even more than that girl he used to like. She just made fun of him and called him Glick!"

"Glick?" I asked, puzzled. Then I understood. "A girl he liked made fun of him by calling him that? So that's why he gets so angry when someone calls him Glick!"

Lenny looked angry at himself for letting that information slip out. "Yeah," he admitted reluctantly. "Glick was the name of some creepy character on an old TV show. But I'll kill you if you tell anyone that. The point still is that Nicky was in pain because of what you did to him."

"But I didn't do it to hurt him," I insisted. "It just had to end!" I sighed. I wasn't getting through to him. "Look, when you and Ellen broke up, I'm sure you hurt her. She won't even come around anymore because of all the names you call her."

"Ellen?" He laughed bitterly. "That was an entirely different situation. We were fighting like crazy before we broke up. She had it coming to her. Nicky is a different story. He was never mean to you. I'm his friend and I saw how hurt he was because of the rotten way you treated him!"

"That's easy to say from your point of view!" I shouted. "I'm Ellen's friend, and I saw how hurt she was! Therefore, I should start being nasty to you. If we went on like that, everyone would hate everyone else. We'd have no crowd at all!" I jumped up from my seat and furiously began gathering up my things.

Lenny grabbed my arm and pulled me back down. "Sit down, spitfire!" He laughed. "Did you know your eyes get bigger when you're angry?" I struggled, but he wouldn't let me go.

"Will you calm down and listen to me for a minute, Linda? You're the one who started this conversation!"

I glared at him but stayed in my seat. "Okay," I said, finally. "Let's hear your words of wisdom."

He looked at me and laughed again. I hated to be laughed at. I was on the verge of getting up once more when he grew serious. "You're right," he admitted. "In any breakup, someone's bound to get hurt. It's unavoidable, no matter how good your intentions are. All these feelings are just part of growing up."

Lenny smiled and looked straight into my eyes. As he did, his eyes filled with so much emotion and understanding that something connected between us, something that I had never felt with a boy before.

It was as if I suddenly saw him as a person, with all his hopes and hurts. I knew then that the loudmouth Lenny was just a front for a lot of feeling underneath. For that brief moment I knew him. At the same time I felt that he knew me.

The moment passed. I dropped my eyes self-consciously. I heard him laugh.

"I guess you're not so bad for a punky little girl!"

I glared at him angrily. Then I laughed, too. At least he was saying it now in an affectionate way.

I wondered what it would be like to be Lenny Lipoff's girlfriend. He had ways about him that would probably drive me crazy. But Lenny had depth, and he could be more fun than anyone else in the crowd. It would be a wonderful feeling to have a boyfriend again. Could Lenny be a possibility?

Any thoughts along these lines about Lenny were

quickly eliminated once we got to the beach. Lenny paid absolutely no attention to me. He divided his time between eating an enormous amount of hot dogs, hamburgers, knishes, french fries, and sodas on the boardwalk; playing games at the amusement area; and flirting on the beach with Renee Berkley!

This was the first time Renee had come somewhere with our crowd unaccompanied by Louie. He had to go somewhere with his parents and couldn't make it to the beach.

It was also her first time to reveal her body in a bathing suit. This really caused a stir with the boys. The tight sweaters she usually wore were bad enough. In a bathing suit, even I had to admit she was dynamite. She wore a one-piece suit that pulled her in at the waistline and pushed her out on top. The boys' eyes kept focusing on the area where she didn't quite fit into the suit.

It was disgusting to see the boys hanging around her, devising ways to get close enough to peek down her suit. But as angry as I was, it was nothing compared to the way Fran and Roz were feeling. Dan and Sheldon seemed to forget that they had girlfriends. They hovered around Renee like flies.

Renee was eating it up. She fluttered her made-up lashes and arched her back to show off.

"Aren't you going into the ocean, Renee?" I asked. "The waves are rough, and it's fun to jump them."

"Oh, I wouldn't dream of going into the water!" She tilted her face to get the best angle of the sun. "I'll just sit here and work on my tan!"

"Suit yourself," I shrugged. "Anyone for the water? I'm going in!"

Fran and Roz joined me. As we walked toward the ocean, we heard screams from the blanket. Lenny, Danny, Sheldon, and Norman had grabbed Renee. They were carrying her, struggling, to the water!

"Should we rescue her?" Roz asked.

"No! Let her get what she deserves!" I answered. I put my toe into the water. "The ocean is like ice this early in the season."

"I hope her precious hairdo is ruined for good!" said Fran.

We watched the boys carrying Renee. They seemed to be trying to hold on to her as long as they could. Renee was laughing and screaming. At last we had the satisfaction of seeing her tossed into the icy waves.

She came up sputtering. "My hair!" she shrieked. She shook her head, sending droplets of water flying all over. "I just washed and blew it dry this morning!"

"Who in the world would wash and blow dry their hair before going to the beach?" I laughed. "Now that Renee's dripping wet, maybe she won't look so good to the boys after all."

"Oh, no?" Roz said with a frown. "Look again!"

I followed her gaze to where Renee was emerging from the ocean. The wetness had made her suit cling even more. It emphasized how well-endowed she was by nature. In comparison, Roz, Fran, and I looked like little children!

Renee wiggled her way back to the blanket. The boys went panting after her. Lenny even ran ahead to bring her a towel. He put his arm around her as he draped the towel around her shoulders. He had this longing look on his face.

The whole scene made me absolutely ill! To think I had even allowed myself to consider liking Lenny Lipoff. I must have been out of my mind!

Chapter Fifteen

It was a good thing that I was almost finished with my last final exam. Because when Ms. Bouton stopped at my desk and told me she wanted to speak to me after the exam was over, I could hardly concentrate on the remaining questions. Then I had to wait until everyone else finished and left the room before I could find out what she wanted.

"Come up here to my desk, Linda," Ms. Bouton said finally. "I'm just about finished marking your exam."

I stood up, knocking my looseleaf to the floor. My fingers shook as I picked up the papers that had scattered all over. I had no idea why Ms. Bouton had singled me out this way. As far as I knew, my grades were all good. What had gone wrong?

"It's nothing bad," Ms. Bouton alleviated my fears as I approached her desk. "I marked your final now because I wanted to be sure. As I thought, it's over ninety, so you've earned an A for this term again. In fact, I've received your grades from all your teachers. You've got another straight A term, which qualifies you for the top ten of the eighth grade class!''

"Really? That's terrific!" I was overjoyed at the news. Here I thought I would have to wait until Monday night's final assembly to find out if I had made it, and now . . .

"It is, except for one thing." Ms. Bouton interrupted my thoughts.

"What's that?"

"Your club participation. Although I have you down as belonging to the service club, the supervising teacher from the Manhattan School, Miss Wise, never sent in the verification papers. Until I get them, I can't give you official credit for the club. And if you don't have credit for at least one club, that automatically disqualifies you for the top ten. That means that Jan Zieglebaum and Samantha Milken will be the two students from our class to be honored at the final assembly.''

"But Jan was in the service club, too" I protested. "How come her verification came through?"

"It didn't. But that doesn't matter for her because she's already gotten credit for being in the art club. And besides, Jan slipped this term in one of her classes, which makes her average slightly lower than yours and Samantha's. So, if you get your club verification, it will be you and Samantha who are on top.''

"Me and Samantha?" I repeated blankly.

"Samantha and I," Ms. Bouton corrected. "We

can't have one of our top ten students using incorrect grammar! Now, what I'd like you to do, Linda, is run over to the Manhattan School right now. Go see Miss Wise and get the verification papers signed. I'll give you a new set in case she misplaced the originals.

"I'm not leaving school for another hour. If you bring the papers back to me before then, I'll see that the information gets put on your record in time to have you counted in for the top ten. Now remember, Linda. I'm telling you this in confidence. You're not to repeat this information to anyone—especially not to Jan or Samantha."

"Oh no, I won't," I promised. "Especially not to Jan or Samantha."

I walked to the Manhattan School in a daze, my fingers clutched tightly around the papers I needed to have signed. The papers that would verify my participation in the service club. The papers that would put me up there in the top ten students in the whole eighth grade—the goal I had worked for all year. I was going to be honored in front of all the parents at the final assembly.

I guess I should have been happy about this turn of events, but I wasn't. The fact that Jan wasn't going to be up there with me ruined everything.

I still felt guilty about what had happened with Jan. I felt terrible because she was no longer a part of the Gruesome Four. She never hung around with us and the boys after school. She never came to any of our parties. Jan's mother had gotten her way completely.

We had been reduced to the Gruesome Three, and I hadn't been able to do a thing about it.

But what bothered me the most was that I would be leaving Jan in order to go to Bronx Technology next year. Now on top of everything, I was giving it to her again. I was about to bump her out of the top ten.

I was so engrossed in my thoughts as I entered the Manhattan School that I didn't watch where I was going. I ran right into someone standing in the front lobby.

"Oops. Excuse me," I apologized. Then I looked and saw it was Jeremy. Just my luck! I had managed to basically avoid him since turning him down for the prom, and now here I was practically knocking him over! I held my breath, hoping he wouldn't realize it was me.

I should have known better. "Linda!" he said immediately. "What are you doing here?"

I don't know what got into me. I guess I just really needed someone to talk to, and Jeremy was there at the right time. Anyhow, I found myself blurting out the whole story of Jan, Bronx Technology, and the top ten at Huntington.

"So, what it all comes down to is that if you get these papers signed now, you're in and Jan is out," said Jeremy.

"Exactly. And Jan won't get first shot at picking her classes next year, which is really important to her." I shook my head. "You know, Jeremy, I had it all planned out in my mind. The way Jan and I would get up together in front of the whole assembly to receive our honors. It would almost make up for the fact that I was leaving her and going to Tech. But things never seem to work out the way you plan them to."

"No," he said with a pained look on his face. "They don't seem to, do they?"

I flushed as I realized what he was talking about—his relationship with me that hadn't worked out at all. But I guess I really deserved that one. I couldn't even find the words to answer him.

Then his face brightened. "But you never know, Linda. Sometimes the way they do work out turns out to be for the best. Take the girl I wound up bringing to the prom. She was in my English class all year, but I never paid much attention to her until you turned me down. Then I discovered she was really worth knowing. What seemed to be a bad thing turned out to be the start of something good."

"Really? I'm so glad to hear that, Jeremy."

He smiled. "Well, whatever your decision is—I have the feeling it'll be best for you, too."

I sighed. "Maybe. But I don't see how. But anyhow, Jeremy—"

"Yes?"

"Just thanks for listening. I'll really miss having a friend like you." I took his hand and squeezed it. Then I walked off to bring my papers to Miss Wise.

My birthday, like the end of the school year, fell in late June. That weekend, Danny threw a party that was supposed to be in my honor. It was a nice gesture, but with me the only girl in the crowd to have no boyfriend, I would have been better off staying at home.

The party turned into a kissing session, and I had no one to kiss. Danny and Fran and Roz and Sheldon went into the living room and sat on the sofa. Louie and Renee plopped down on the rug. So did Nicky and Ellen, who had surprised everyone recently by getting together as a new couple.

I was miserable. I was left with Norman and Lenny. We stared at one another for a few minutes.

"This party stinks," Lenny said bluntly. "I'm leaving." He took one last look at Ellen and Nicky, who were kissing; then he walked out the door.

I was angry at Lenny for being so cruel, but I knew he was right. This was a party for couples. It was dumb for me to hang around with everyone paired-off and kissing. But, then again, this was my birthday. Unlike Lenny, I couldn't leave because the party was given for me.

There I was with everyone around me having a great time kissing. I sat on the window with Norman and played dumb games. I stuck out my hands, palms together. I tried to pull them back before he could slap me with his hands. If I did, he had to stick out his hands, and I got to try to slap him.

It hurt when he slapped me. Each time he hit me, I would get mad. That made me hit even harder when it was my turn.

"Ow!" he said, finally. "I've had enough of this game!"

I sighed and looked around the room. I had had

enough of the entire scene! Even in the dark, I could see how Louie was enjoying himself kissing Renee. Watching them brought back all the pain I had felt when he rejected me.

I looked away to Nicky and Ellen. It was strange how they had found each other. I wondered if Nicky ever thought about me at all. It sure didn't look that way to watch him with Ellen. I didn't matter to anyone. I bet no one would notice if I left the party.

"Norman," I whispered. "I'm going home. Tell everyone good-bye for me." I headed for the door.

At that moment, I heard a key click in the door. Danny's parents must have decided to come home early!

"The lights! Put on the lights!" I called. Norman ran to flick them on, but it was too late. Mr. and Mrs. Kopler could see just what had been going on!

They called Danny into the kitchen. The rest of us sat in his room and waited. We could hear the screams coming through the walls. Norman tried to crack a joke, but no one laughed.

Mrs. Kopler came storming into the room. "Get out of here!" she yelled in a high-pitched voice. She was a small fragile woman, but she had a temper. "Get out of my house and never come back!"

Danny was right behind her. He grabbed his mother roughly by the arm and shoved her aside. I was frightened. What was wrong with Danny to treat his mother that way?

"I'll tell my friends when to leave!" he shouted. "Let's get out of here, gang!"

We were only too happy to leave. As we rushed through the door, Mr. Kopler got into the act. He lunged after Danny and tried to grab him. Danny jumped aside and ran down the stairs.

We all went into the candy store. Danny kept marching back and forth, mumbling under his breath. No one had the courage to ask him what had happened.

Finally, Fran went over and put her hand on his arm. "What happened, Danny?" she asked. "Why did you flip out at your mother?"

He shook her off angrily. "They can't do it! I'll just refuse! I won't let them!" He smashed his fist down on the counter.

"Hey you kids! Out of here!" Harry, the candy store owner, hollered. "No one is buying anything! Get out into the street where you belong!"

No one was in the mood to argue. We left the store and stood on the corner. It wasn't a good feeling to be thrown out twice in one night. Some birthday celebration this was!

Danny seemed a bit calmer. I tried approaching him. "Come on, Danny. Will you please tell us what's going on here?"

Danny looked at everyone, his eyes full. "They're moving!" he sputtered. "They're sick of having kids up at the house. They want to get me away from the crowd. They took an apartment clear across the city in Forest Hills. I've got until the end of July. Then, I'll be gone!"

We stood speechless. Fran began to cry. I think I felt worse than she did. True, Danny was her boyfriend, but to me he was like a brother. Whenever I needed someone to talk to, Danny had been right there, in the apartment above mine. What would I do without him now?

"It can't be true," I moaned. "We can't let it happen. We have to think of something!"

Chapter Sixteen

IT WAS THE final assembly at Huntington. The graduating seniors put on their senior skit and sang their class song. Then there was the "Move-up" ceremony for the eighth graders who were entering the upper division. The highlight of the ceremony was the calling up to the stage of the girls who had made it to the top ten.

The auditorium was darkened. The stage was lit only by spotlights. Dr. Lilienthal began reading the names—the two girls from each of the five eighth grade classes who had earned this highest honor.

I found my heart hammering wildly when she got to our class. I guess I was hoping against hope that somehow something had happened to change things around so they would work out the way I wanted them to—with both Jan and me up there receiving the awards from our class.

"Samantha Milken!" Dr. Lilienthal announced.

There. It was over. Samantha, in one of her medieval-styled dresses with puffed sleeves and a tight bodice walked triumphantly onto the stage.

"Jan Zieglebaum!" said Dr. Lilienthal.

"Wow! I can't believe it!" I heard Jan exclaim. For I knew that once she saw her report card, Jan had figured she was out of the running for sure.

Jan hopped out of her seat and ran joyously up the steps to the stage. The audience laughed aloud. Little Jan looked so funny, laughing and crying at the same time as Dr. Lilienthal handed her the award.

I couldn't help laughing, too. After all, I didn't really need any dumb awards from Huntington, anyhow. I was really glad that I had decided, at the last minute, that the verification papers were best left unsigned.

Once school had ended, we went on a big campaign to keep the Koplers from moving. We painted signs and picketed the building. We sent cards begging them to stay. Since I had always gotten along with Danny's parents, I tried personally to get them to change their minds.

Nothing helped. We became resigned to the sad fact that by the end of July, Danny would be gone.

Things changed in the summertime. Some kids went away. Others worked or went to summer school. But whenever we could, we would hang around the park wall. Teenagers from all over the neighborhood gathered there in the evening.

I loved it. I wanted to be part of that wonderful

feeling of belonging forever. The only thing I still needed was a boyfriend.

Roz went away with her parents for two weeks in the middle of July. Sheldon seemed lost without her. He hung around the wall, moping and drooping.

"I bet you'll be glad when Roz comes home tomorrow," I told him. "Now you know how I feel. It's awful not to have someone!"

Sheldon walked me home from the wall that night. It was nine o'clock, the time when the wall was first getting lively, but I had to be home. No matter how much I pleaded with my parents, if there was no party, my curfew was at nine. I felt like I was being robbed of some of the best moments of my life.

"You know I never realized it before Roz left," Sheldon admitted. "There's such an emptiness when you're alone. We're going to do something to fix your boyfriend situation, Linda."

"Like what?"

"Just be patient a little while longer," he laughed, flipping his hair back out of his eyes. "I'm going to hit upon the right boyfriend for you real soon."

But when Roz came back, Sheldon had other things to worry about. She had met someone she liked up in the country. When she came home, she was no longer sure of how she felt about Sheldon.

Instead of running into his arms when she saw him, she pulled back bashfully.

"What's wrong, Roz?" He had a hurt look on his face.

"I don't know, Sheldon," she answered. "I guess it's just strange to be back. Come on, Linda. Let's go for a walk!" She dragged me towards her house.

"I'm so confused, Linda," she confided. "I guess I still like Sheldon, but it's not like before. In the country, with Barry, it was like magic. We had such a wonderful time together. He lives in Boston, so I'll probably never see him again. But if I really like Sheldon, how could I feel that way about Barry?"

We stopped walking when we got to the back of the park. We sat on the grass and watched the Hudson River flow by. The air shimmered as it rose from the heated sidewalks.

"I think you just answered your own question, Roz," I said.

"I did? How?"

"When you said that being in the country with Barry was just like magic. It's true, you know. It happened to me when I was away last summer. There was a boy there I thought I was crazy about. He called me once in the city, and I didn't even want to see him again."

"So?"

"So, I think that's what's happening to you, only you don't know it yet. You live here, not in the country. When you come back and the magic goes away, you re left to face the real you again. Sometimes it's hard to adjust to."

Roz sighed and picked herself up from the grass. "Maybe you're right, Linda. But I'm still not sure if I like Sheldon."

"Just don't go rushing into breaking up with him," I told her. "I bet tomorrow you'll feel like your old self again!"

"I hope so," she said doubtfully. "See you tomorrow!"

Roz didn't come out that night. Sheldon, Lenny, and I sat by ourselves on the park wall. It seemed that Lenny was always around whenever people were having problems with their love life. It was too bad he couldn't straighten out his own.

"Don't worry, Sheldon." I finished telling him my theories about Roz. "I'm sure that by tomorrow she'll adjust to being back in the city again. Just give her time. It's you she really cares about."

"Do you think so?" he asked doubtfully.

"I know so." I wanted to make Sheldon feel good. He was really one of my favorite people. I was the one who had originally pointed him out to Roz as being cute. I felt responsible for getting them together in the first place. I was going to do all I could to get them back together now.

"I have to admit Linda's right, Sheldon." Lenny agreed. "Don't get upset now. See how Roz acts tomorrow. If she doesn't come around, you break up with her first!"

"Lenny!" I glared at him. "Thanks for being so helpful!"

"I'm only trying to cheer the guy up." Lenny laughed. "Let's go down to the candy store, Sheldon. I'll buy you a soda. You can come too, Linda," he said as an afterthought. "It's my treat!"

I glanced at my watch. It was almost nine. "I can't." I frowned. "I have to return to prison. Curfew time, you know!"

I walked with them as far as my house. "Take good care of Sheldon tonight, Lenny," I joked. "We want him to make it till tomorrow!"

As I had predicted, Roz and Sheldon got back together the next day. For my role as mediator, I won Sheldon's undying gratitude.

That night, we were sitting alone on the park wall before the other kids came out. "Remember when I told you I'd find the right boyfriend for you, Linda?" he asked.

"Yeah. So have you materialized him from thin air?"

Sheldon laughed. "Well, the funniest part of it is that the answer has been right in front of our noses, but we just didn't see it until now. But now that you've both been so helpful getting me back together with Roz, it's obvious that you were meant for one another all along!" He looked very satisfied with himself for having made this statement.

But I wasn't satisfied. "Sheldon! You're talking in riddles. Will you please tell me who this person is?"

"Why, Lenny, of course!" He beamed.

I stared at him. "Lenny? You don't mean Lenny Lipoff?"

"Why not? You need a boyfriend. He needs a girlfriend. You're both great people. You'd make a perfect couple!"

I blinked, trying to absorb what Sheldon had said.

Lenny Lipoff! Of course the thought of liking him had entered my mind before, but I had always put it right back out again. Lenny was such a wise guy, so wild, crazy, and unpredictable. He was capable of getting me angrier than anyone else I knew.

But then again, I could never stay angry at Lenny for very long—no one could. And when Lenny was nice, he was really wonderful. He was such fun to be with, so full of life, and so funny—he could have the whole crowd laughing in no time at all.

But more than that, Lenny had feelings. I remembered how caring he had been the night Louie had broken up with me. Just talking to Lenny had made me feel so much better. He had been there for Nicky and Sheldon when they had problems, too.

Maybe it was all the trouble Lenny had at home that made him so sensitive to others. But whatever the reason, it was a great quality that Lenny had. I remembered now that flash of understanding that had passed between us the time we were riding in the train to Rockaway. I had never felt anything like that with another boy.

Underneath it all, I had probably liked Lenny all along, but I had never wanted to admit it. I guess that was because Lenny was so difficult, and I had been afraid of getting hurt again after what had happened with Louie.

I was still afraid.

"What do you think?" Sheldon smiled. "Am I a genius, or am I a genius?"

"I don't know, Sheldon. I'm almost afraid to get

involved with Lenny. You never know what he is going to do next."

"Hey—don't worry about that. You can calm him down if anyone can. Just tell me, you do like him, don't you?"

"I guess so," I admitted. "At least I would like him if he liked me. We don't know that, do we?"

"He likes you. He likes you."

"How do you know that, Sheldon? Did he tell you?"

"Not exactly. But I'm Lenny's best friend. I know what he wants even before he does. Just remember tomorrow's date, Linda. On July twenty-sixth you're going to have yourself a boyfriend!"

By the time I went out the next day, rumors had already spread around the neighborhood that Lenny and I were a couple.

"Linda, I heard the news! That's terrific!" Roz greeted me at the wall.

"What news?"

"About you and Lenny, of course! Sheldon told me he likes you!"

"I'm glad Sheldon told you that. But it means nothing until I hear it from Lenny, himself."

We all went up to Danny's in the afternoon. It was one of the last days we would have at his house before he moved. Packed cartons were already stacked in the corner of his room.

The boys started playing cards. The bell rang and Lenny came in. My heart beat faster when I saw him.

I really did like him. If only the rumors were true. If only he did want me for his girlfriend!

"Come sit with me, Linda," he said. "Be my lucky charm!"

I sat with him on the chair and felt my whole body start to tingle. I watched his profile as he concentrated on his cards. He was so involved in everything he did.

"Look at the newlyweds," Norman commented. "They sure look cute together!"

Lenny laughed as he threw out a card. What Norman said didn't seem to bother him at all. He stayed with me for the rest of the afternoon. He acted so nice that my hopes rose. But he never said anything specific about liking me.

Roz and Fran came down with me to my house. "Do you like him?" they both asked as soon as we were alone.

I sighed. "Yeah. I have to admit I like him even more than I thought I would. I can tell I could really fall for Lenny if I let myself. But I'm not going to—not until I know how he feels about me. So right now, we're still at base zero!"

When I came out after supper, the kids at the park told me my friends were waiting for me at the Haven Avenue wall. That wall overlooked the Hudson River and the George Washington Bridge.

They were all standing in a group when I got there: Roz, Fran, Sheldon, Danny, and Lenny. They stopped talking when they saw me. I knew it was me they had been talking about.

This made me angry. It was one thing to suggest that Lenny and I might be a good couple. It was another thing for my friends to get together behind my back to try to fix me up!

I stopped short. I would show them all that no one was going to make my decisions for me. I turned around and started stalking back up the block.

"Linda!" Lenny called after me. "Where are you going?"

"Back to the park," I called back. "Where no one is standing around arranging my life!"

"Oh come on," he laughed. He came over and grabbed my arm. "I promise that no one will do any arranging. I just want to talk to you."

"Not in front of an audience, you're not!" I gestured to the group at the wall.

"No, of course not. I'll get rid of them," he agreed. "How about leaving Linda and me alone for a while?" he said to the crowd. "We'll meet you later, back at the park."

I watched my friends walking away. I was afraid to look at Lenny, so I turned to gaze at the river. The sun was starting to set, and it had turned the sky bright shades of red and orange. The colors reflected in the water and glinted off the great steel bridge.

My heart was racing. I couldn't believe how much I had come to like Lenny once I had begun to let myself. It was scary. It was something I wasn't sure I could control.

I turned to him and found he was looking at me. As our eyes met, I felt that special chemistry surging between us. We stood there like that, just staring into one another's eyes.

"Well?" I said, finally breaking the spell.

"Well, what?" He looked startled.

"Well, I thought you wanted to talk to me."

"Oh. Yeah, sure." He hoisted himself up on the wall and patted the spot next to him. "How about sitting here so we can talk?"

"Okay." I climbed up next to him and waited for him to speak.

He took a deep breath. "Well, I suppose you know about all the rumors going around today about our being a couple."

"Uh-huh," I admitted. My hopes were rising.

"Well—uh—it seems Sheldon told me something you said to him the other night. Remember what it was?"

"I said a lot of things that night," I answered. No matter how much I liked Lenny, I wasn't going to commit myself unless he did. "What, specifically, are you talking about?"

His eyes sparkled. "I'll give you a hint. Sheldon said that if Lenny *blank blank blank,* then Linda *blank blank blank.*"

Of course I knew exactly what he meant, but I pretended not to. We fooled around, and I guessed all sorts of wild possibilities before I admitted to what really went in the blanks: "If Lenny would like Linda, then Linda would like Lenny!"

"In that case, let's make some changes in that statement," he said, suddenly. "It might have taken

Sheldon to call it to my attention, but the feeling was there for a long time. You see, Lenny does like Linda!"

When he said that, I was filled with this warm, wonderful glow. He had put into words just what I was feeling. I smiled up at him. "And Linda does like Lenny." I practically breathed the words. Then I waited to see what he would say next.

But Lenny seemed to know instinctively it was not words that were called for here. His hand reached out and clasped mine. Then, before I knew what was happening, his lips met mine in a kiss so intense it took my breath away.

He let his arm slip around me, and we sat there like that, watching the sun set on the river. I snuggled up next to him, fitting against his body as if I had always belonged there and would forevermore. My heart was pounding so hard I was afraid he would hear it.

I could scarcely believe it. I had a boyfriend. And not just any boyfriend. I had Lenny Lipoff, the person who could make me feel better than anyone else.

I would make Lenny feel good, too. I would calm him down, bring out the best in him, and he would bring out the best in me. It would work out for us—I knew it would. The way everything had come together like this—it was something that was meant to be.

We were going to have the best relationship of them all!

ABOUT THE AUTHOR

LINDA LEWIS was graduated from City College of New York and received her masters degree in Special Education. *We Love Only Older Boys* is her third novel. She has also written two other books about Linda: *We Hate Everything But Boys* and *Is There Life After Boys?* Recently she moved from New York to Lauderdale-by-the-Sea, Florida. She is married and has two children.